THE ADVENTURES OF TINTIN

KING OTTOKAR'S SCEPTRE

eih bennek eih blâvek

Little, Brown and Company
New York   Boston

Original Album: *King Ottokar's Sceptre*
Renewed Art Copyright © 1946, 1974 by Casterman, Belgium
Text Copyright © 1975 by Egmont UK Limited

Translated by Leslie Lonsdale-Cooper and Michael Turner

Additional Material
Art Copyright © Hergé/Moulinsart 2011
Text Copyright © Moulinsart 2011

www.casterman.com
www.tintin.com

Little, Brown and Company
Hachette Book Group
237 Park Avenue, New York, NY 10017
Visit our website at www.lb-kids.com

The publisher is not responsible for websites (or their content) that are not owned by the publisher.

First Edition: December 2011

ISBN: 978-0-316-13383-8
2011921034
2
SC
Printed in China
L.10EIFN001276.B002

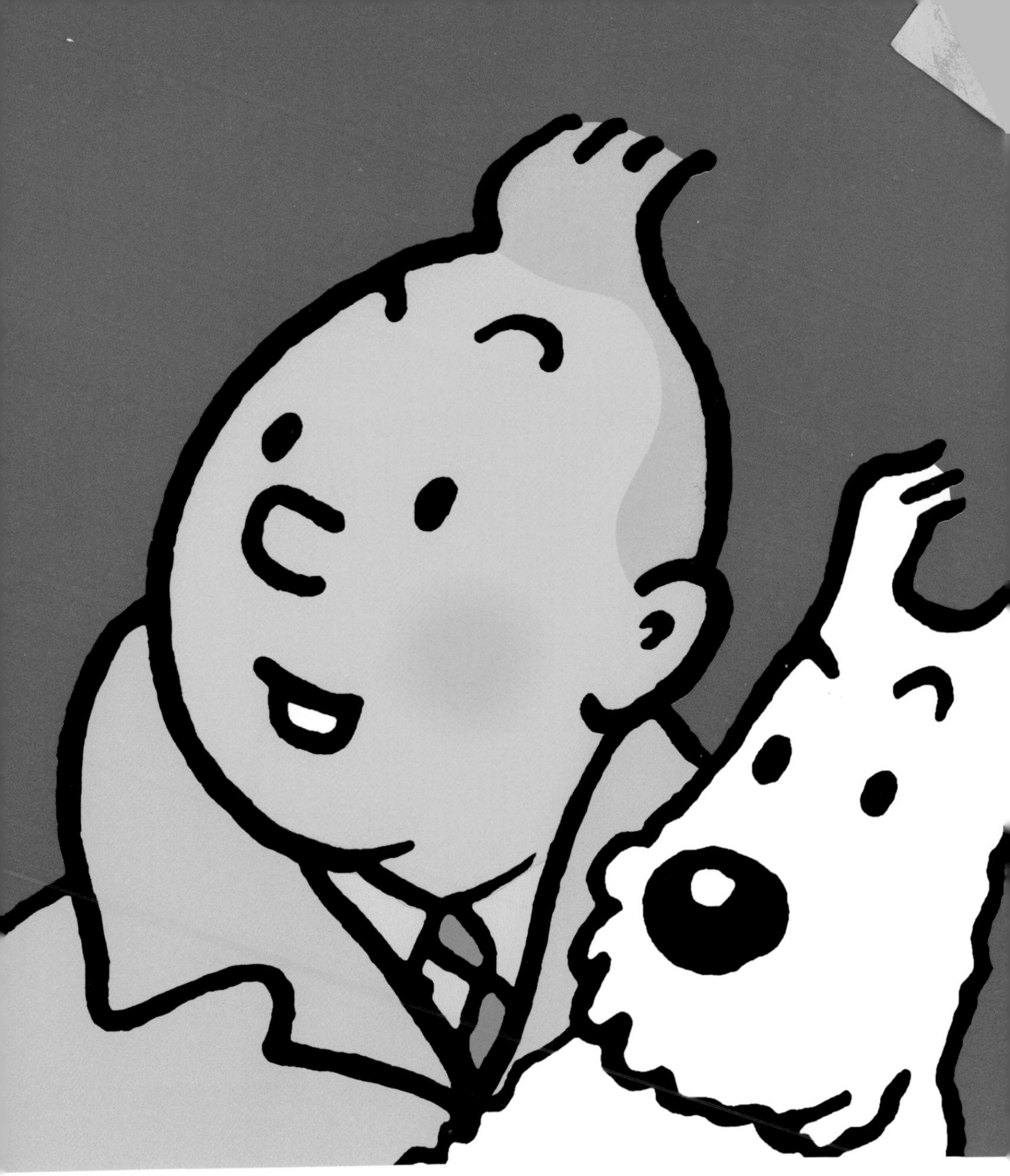

Tintin and Snowy

Helpful Tintin doesn't think twice before returning a lost briefcase to its owner; his faithful dog, Snowy, knows that Tintin's good will often leads to new adventures!

Professor Alembick

Professor Hector Alembick is an expert in the study of wax seals. Little does the unsuspecting professor know that he is also the key to a ruthless plot to depose the King of Syldavia.

Thomson and Thompson

Although the dimwitted police detectives are determined to help Tintin, it is not long before they are falling off motorcycles and being tricked by suspicious parcels!

King Muskar XII

The just and noble King of Syldavia comes from an established lineage of great leaders. Will King Muskar manage to overcome plotters determined to force him from his throne?

Trovik

A key member of the criminal organization planning to overthrow
the King of Syldavia, Trovik coordinates multiple attempts
to get Tintin out of the way…permanently!

Bianca Castafiore

The first time Tintin meets the opera singer from Milan,
Bianca Castafiore manages to save the reporter from an ambush.
But can Tintin survive her ear-piercing opera arias?

Colonel Boris

The trusted aide to King Muskar XII, scheming Boris uses his position to trap Tintin. But the villain doesn't know who he is up against!

KING OTTOKAR'S SCEPTRE

Let's sit down on this bench for a minute.

Hello, someone has left his brief-case behind.

I can't see anybody . . .

Perhaps I ought to open it? The owner's name might be inside.

Here it is! . . . 'Hector Alembick, 24, Flyaway Road'.

That's not far. I'll take it back.

You're making a mistake, Tintin! . . . No good ever comes of getting mixed up in other people's business.

FLYAWAY ROAD

Professor Alembick? Third floor, first door on the right . . .

24

RAT TAT TAT

Come in!

Oh, good-evening, Mrs Piggott. Put it all on the little table, will you?

It's not Mrs Piggott, Professor. I've brought back your brief-case.

What? . . .

My brief-case?

Ssh! Someone's just come to see him . . .

How very kind of you to return it. I'm especially grateful, as the text of the paper I am reading to the I.S.A. Congress tonight is in there.

The I.S.A.?

I.S.A.: International Sigillographical Association.

Sigi . . . what?

Sigillography. Do you mean you've never heard of it? It's the science concerned with the study of seals. It's extremely interesting and . . . A cigarette?

No thank you: I don't smoke.

Yes, sigillography is an absorbing study. One look at my collection will convince you.

?

Oh, good gracious! I'm so sorry! I have a dreadful habit of dropping my cigarette ends about!

This is one of the rarest items in my collection: the seal of Charlemagne. Here is the seal of Edward the Confessor, and next to it one which belonged to Gradenigo, Doge of Venice. And here's another fine specimen: an intaglio ring from the Saxon period.

. . . And this is a very unusual seal, which I found quite by chance in Prague. It is the seal of Ottokar IV, King of Syldavia . . .

Oh? . . .

It is one of the few seals we know of from that country. But there must be others, and I am going to Syldavia to study the problem on the spot.

The Syldavian Ambassador, an old friend of mine, has promised to give me letters of introduction. I hope I shall be allowed to go through the historic national archives. A cigarette? . . .

No, thank you . . . And when are you leaving?

As soon as I have found a secretary. At least, rather more than a secretary; I really need someone to take care of all the details of my journey, like hotels, passports, luggage and so on.

But I see that you have become interested in sigillography too. Let me have your name and address and I will send you my booklet: 'How to become a sigillographer.'

How very kind of you . . .

He's going . . . Quick, meet him on the stairs . . .

Steady! . . . Here he comes!

CLICK

That's a funny place to put a watch right . . .

Got it! . . . Wonderful, the way a miniature camera can be hidden in a watch . . .

Here! . . .

We'll develop the picture right away.

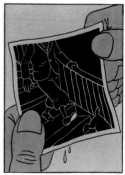

!?

Is it OK?

Bother! I've left my book at Professor Alembick's flat.

Anyway, we know his name is Tintin.

2nd FLOOR

?

Tintin! ... Tintin! ... You know that a name by itself won't do ... We must have a photograph!

Well, I've had enough ... I'm off ... If anyone wants me, I'm at the 'KLOW'! ... Goodbye! ...

Goodbye!

24

This is all very mysterious ... Let's follow him.

- KLOW -

SYLDAVIAN RESTAURANT

LOW -

RESTAUR

Well, well! 'Syldavian Restaurant'. The plot thickens!

Let's go in!

KLOW

Hello? ... Where's he gone?

A customer! ...

④

Er . . . I'd like . . . something to eat . . . please . . .

Will you take a seat, sir? . . .

What would you like, sir? . . .

Er . . . bring me . . . er . . . a 'szlaszeck' with mushrooms . . . and a glass of 'szpradj' . . .

But I'd like a wash first . . .

The cloakroom is at the end of the passage.

. . . As for Professor Alembick, we'll have to wait for a day or two, until he's got the papers from the Embassy . . .

Ahem!

At the end of the passage, sir . . .

I'm sorry, I misunderstood.

Did he catch me listening at the door?

. . . and he was listening outside the door! He's a young chap with a funny tuft of hair . . . There's a dog with him . . .

I'll bet a thousand khors it's the fellow Sporovitch tried to photograph! . . .

Where's Snowy got to? . . .

TING

TING

TING

My bill, please . . .

In a moment, sir . . .

?

·KLOW·
SYLDAVIAN RESTAURANT
3B, NIGHTINGALE ROAD
PROP: J. KNOSZVITCH

1 Szlaszeck danj . . . 1·20
. . . . ·60
1 Szpäs . . . . . . 1·80
. . . . ·18
Servis 10% . . . . 1·98

Danger awaits the one who dares
To poke his nose in others' affairs
~ SYLDAVIAN PROVERB ~

What does this mean?

What, sir? . . . Oh, yes . . . Don't you know the old Syldavian custom, sir? . . . In restaurants in my country there's always a proverb or a short motto on the bill.

Oh, really?

Yes, sir. Rather nice, isn't it? . . . Thank you, just right . . . I hope you enjoyed your meal, sir? . . .

Very much, thank you. Your 'szlaszeck' was excellent. How do you make it?

Ah, it's one of our specialities: the hind leg of a young dog in Syldavian sauce . . .

SNOWY!

SNOWY! SNOWY!

?

Ah, there you are! . . . Where have you been hiding?

I hope you will come again, sir.

Ha! ha! ha! We shan't see him again in a hurry!

SERVICE

Well I'm . . . !

Odd! All very odd! . . .

HIC

HIC

A few minutes later . . .

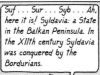
Suf . . . Sur . . . Syb . . . Ah, here it is! Syldavia: a State in the Balkan Peninsula. In the XIIth century Syldavia was conquered by the Bordurians.

RRRRING
RRRRING
RRRRING

Hello? . . . Yes, it's me . . . Yes of course it's me . . . I . . . Who are you? . . . What? You'll tell me later? . . . Can you come and see me? What about? . . . Oh! . . . All right, I'll expect you about half past eight . . . . Goodbye . . .

A man with a foreign accent, with something very important to tell me . . . ?

HIC

In 1275 the people of Syldavia rose against the Bordurians, and in 1277 the revolutionary leader, Baron Almaszout, was proclaimed King. He adopted the title of Ottokar the First, but should not be confused with Premysl Ottokar the First, the duke who became King of Bohemia in the XIIth century.

HIC

Twenty past eight. My mysterious foreigner should soon be here.

TINTIN

RRRING

HIC

?

No one there!

Let's look out of the window! . . .

I say, Tintin, my hiccups have gone!

I really must get this window mended! . . .

SMASH

No one there, of course! . . .

I'd better do something about this poor chap.

I must get him on to the sofa.

You know he said his door would always be open to us . . .

I'd better shut the door first . . .

You have a fine way of welcoming people! . . . Oho! What's all this?

Help me to lift him on to the sofa, would you? . . .

Is he . . . dead?

But tell us what happened.

No, he's alive; his heart is beating.

What happened? . . . Well, about an hour ago this man rang up and asked to see me, and I agreed. At half past eight the bell rang; I opened the door and without a word the poor fellow collapsed at my feet . . .

Hmm!

You said, 'without a word' . . . In that case, how do you know that this was the man who telephoned? . . .

I don't know, but it seemed likely . . .

And what about all this evidence of a struggle?

Evidence of a struggle, my foot! The only struggle I had was with the window, which wouldn't open! You aren't trying to say that I knocked this man out?

I didn't say that, but . . .

Excuse me, gentlemen . . .

May I ask what I am doing here? . . .

I rather think I should be asking you that question . . .

To begin with, can you describe your assailant?

My assailant? . . . What assailant?

Now don't try any funny business with us, my friend . . . Come on, what's your name?

I . . . let's see . . . It's really very odd, but I . . . I can't remember! . . .

For the last time, my man, don't try any funny business with us . . . What's your name?

Out with it! . . . And get a move on!

What if he's telling the truth and he really is suffering from amnesia?

What has anaemia to do with it? . . .

Amnesia! . . . He probably had a violent shock that made him lose his memory! It's always happening. If I were you I'd take him to a hospital and let a doctor have a look at him . . .

Hmm! . . . What do you think? . . .

Hmm! . . . We could try . . .

You know, I can't really believe in this magnesia . . .

It's all very odd . . . I just can't make head or tail of this business . . .

Anyway, I'd better get a new window pane put in . . .

Hello, is that the builder? . . . Could you replace a pane of glass for me? Yes . . . Tintin . . . You'll come tonight? . . . Splendid! . . .

RRRRRING

Oh, it's you! Come in.

There . . .

Thanks

Goodnight Mr Tintin. Always glad to help! . . .

Glad to help! . . . Not again for a long time, I hope . . .

!?!?*!

SMASH

(10)

Nobody . . . The street's quite empty . . .

Ah! There's a note tied to this stone . . .

For the last time : mind your own business!

'For the last time' . . . In other words, 'we have already warned you'. But when? . . . Why, that must have been a warning at the 'Klow'. Of course . . . they were Syldavians! I've got an idea! . . . What if I become the professor's secretary and go with him to Syldavia? . . .

Next day . . .
Bad news! . . . That Tintin went to see Professor Alembick this morning and agreed to go with him to Syldavia as his secretary! . . . He's busy getting his passport now. If he goes with the professor our plan is bound to fail! . . .

You'd better leave this to me; I'll see that Tintin doesn't go!

Some hours later . . .
Mr Tintin? . . . He's gone out.

What's that, my boy?

It's a parcel for Mr Tintin.

Give me that. We'll wait for Tintin upstairs, and give him this ourselves . . .

But . . .

That's enough: we're the police!

Look, there's a letter with the parcel . . . Should we open it? . . .

'If you want an explanation of yesterday's events, you will find it in this parcel. A Friend.'

Excellent! . . . What a stroke of luck. Now we shall find something interesting . . .

There are two men waiting in your room; they told me they were from   the police . . .

Oh? . . . Good!

I wonder what they've got to tell me . . .

BOOM

!?

There it goes!

BOOM

?

What have you done? What's happened? . . .

Er . . . there was a parcel for you . . .

. . . and a letter . . . Here: read it . . . We opened the parcel. We heard a 'fizz' and we just had time to throw it away, or it would have blown up in our faces!

Let's get nearer; we can mix with the crowd . . .

A bomb! . . . The cunning scoundrels! . . . They wanted to kill me!

!?

Quick, downstairs! . . . The men who did it are out there! . . .

Hurry! Hurry!

There they are!

It's him!

Quick . . . Start her up!
. . . I'll hold them off!

Look out! . . .

BANG

Give me a gun . . .

BANG

Too late! . . .
They've got
away!

There's a motor bike! . . .
We've got to follow them!

Get going! We're
all set! . . .

To be precise: we're
all set!

Right! . . .

Whatever happens,
hang on tight!

He's alone! . . . We'll fix him! . . . Let him gradually close up on us . . .

We're catching up!

Now we've got 'em! . . .

Now then, jam on the brakes . . . Wham! . . .

⁉

This time I think we've really shaken him off for good.

Where's Snowy? . . . And the others? . . . What's happened to them?

It can't be true! Surely . . . yes, it's them! . . . Where have they come from?

You started off so suddenly that we . . . we couldn't keep up with you. So we commandeered this car. Shall we follow them? . . .

It's no good: they're too far ahead.

I'll leave you here. I must go and pack my things at once. I am going to Syldavia tomorrow.

RRRRING
RRRRING
RRRRING
RRRRING

RRRRING

Hello? . . . Yes . . . Ah, good-evening, Professor . . . Yes, everything is ready for our trip . . . Yes, I have booked seats on the Klow plane . . . We'll meet at the airport in the morning, at 11 o'clock . . .

We go via Prague, yes . . . Well, goodbye till tomorrow, Professor . . . Yes . . . I . . . Hello? . . . Hello? . . . Hello? . . .

Oooooh . . . Help! . . . Help! . . . Aaaaaah! . . .

?

The professor is in danger! Quick! quick! There's not a moment to lose! . . .

I only hope I'm not too late! . . .

?*★¿!!^·*★

Ah! It's you, Tintin. Have you come to help me finish my packing? . . .

I . . . I'm sorry, but I don't understand! . . . I thought I heard you cry out and shout for help . . . So I rushed straight round . . .

Me shouting for help? . . . I'm afraid I don't know what you're talking about.

But it's extraordinary! . . . I can't have been dreaming! . . . I quite definitely heard shouts for help . . .

Next morning . . .

It's very kind of you to come and see me off.

But of course we've come . . .

To be precise: of course . . .

Professor, may I introduce Mr Thomson and Mr Thompson, of the C.I.D. . . . Professor Alembick, sigillographer.

How do you do?

Very well, thank you.

Oh, you've got new hats?

Yes, aren't they smart? . . . Pure English felt, extra-light: only £3-95. Wonderful bargain!

All passengers for Prague, this way please . . .

Well, goodbye, and bon voyage! . . .

And good luck in Syldavia!

Thanks.

Compression! Petrol on! Contact!

Come and look what a pretty picture these sheep make . . . down in that field.

Can you see them, down there?

Yes . . . How tiny they are: you can hardly see them . . .

?

How odd . . .

Are we landing? . . .

Yes: it's Frankfurt. They touch down for a few minutes.

Mr Alembick? There's a telegram for you.

Aha! . . .

Here's some good news . . . The Syldavian government has put a special aircraft at our disposal. Look . . .

'Professor Alembick, passenger aboard aircraft No.573 00-AGE. Frankfurt Airport. Special plane for Klow will meet you at Prague. Stop. Best wishes' . . . It's signed Schzlozitch, Air Minister . . .

Sweets . . . Sandwiches . . . Chocolates . . . Cigarettes . . .

I think they're calling us . . .

All passengers for Prague, please take your seats in the aircraft . . .

00-AGE

It's really very odd . . .

Oh, well, let's forget it and look at this brochure . . .

SYLDAVIA
KINGDOM OF THE BLACK PELICAN

SYLDAVIA
THE KINGDOM OF THE BLACK PELICAN

MONG the many enchanting places which deservedly attract foreign visitors with a love for picturesque ceremony and colourful folklore, there is one small country which, although relatively unknown, surpasses many others in interest. Isolated until modern times because of its inaccessible position, this country is now served by a regular air-line network, which brings it within the reach of all who love unspoiled beauty, the proverbial hospitality of a peasant people, and the charm of medieval customs which still survive despite the march of progress.

This is Syldavia.

Syldavia is a small country in Eastern Europe, comprising two great valleys: those of the river Vladir, and its tributary, the Moltus. The rivers meet at Klow, the capital (122,000 inhabitants). These valleys are flanked by wide plateaux covered with forests, and are surrounded by high, snow-capped mountains. In the fertile Syldavian plains are cornlands and cattle pastures. The subsoil is rich in minerals of all kinds.

Numerous thermal and sulphur springs gush from the earth, the chief centres being at Klow (cardiac diseases) and Kragoniedin (rheumatic complaints).

The total population is estimated to be 642,000 inhabitants.

Syldavia exports wheat, mineral-water from Klow, firewood, horses and violinists.

HISTORY OF SYLDAVIA

Until the VIth century, Syldavia was inhabited by nomadic tribes of unknown origin.

Overrun by the Slavs in the VIth century, the country was conquered in the Xth century by the Turks, who drove the Slavs into the mountains and occupied the plains.

In 1127, Hveghi, leader of a Slav tribe, swooped down from the mountains at the head of a band of partisans and fell upon isolated Turkish villages, putting all who resisted him to the sword. Thus he rapidly became master of a large part of Syldavian territory.

A great battle took place in the valley of the Moltus near Zileheroum, the Turkish capital of Syldavia, between the Turkish army and Hveghi's irregulars.

Enfeebled by long inactivity and badly led by incompetent officers, the Turkish army put up little resistance and fled in disorder.

Having vanquished the Turks, Hveghi was elected king, and given the name Muskar, that is, The Brave (Muskh: 'brave' and Kar: 'king').

The capital, Zileheroum, was renamed Klow, that is, Freetown, (Kloho: 'to free', and Ow: 'town').

Guard at the Royal Treasure House, Klow

A typical fisherman from Dbrnouk (south coast of Syldavia)

◀ *Syldavian peasant on her way to market*

A view of Niedzdrow, in the Vladir valley ▶

THE BATTLE OF ZILEHEROUM
After a XVth century miniature

H.M. King Muskar XII, the present ruler of Syldavia
in the uniform of Colonel of the Guards

him a blow on the head with the sceptre, laying him low and at the same time crying in Syldavian: '*Eih bennek, eih blavek!*', which can be said to mean: 'If you gather thistles, expect prickles'. And turning to his astonished court he said: '*Honi soit qui mal y pense!*'

Then, gazing intently at his sceptre, he addressed it in the following words: 'O Sceptre, thou has saved my life. Be henceforward the true symbol of Syldavian Kingship. Woe to the king who loses thee, for I declare that such a man shall be unworthy to rule thereafter.'

And from that time, every year on St. Vladimir's Day each successor of Ottokar IV has made a great ceremonial tour of his capital.

He bears in his hand the historic sceptre, without which he would lose the right to rule; as he passes, the people sing the famous anthem:

> Syldavians unite!
> Praise our King's might:
> The Sceptre his right!

Right: The sceptre of Ottokar IV

Below: An illuminated page from 'The Memorable Deeds of Ottokar IV', a XIVth century manuscript

Muskar was a wise king who lived at peace with his neighbours, and the country prospered. He died in 1168, mourned by all his subjects.

His eldest son succeeded to the throne with the title of Muskar II.

Unlike his father, Muskar II lacked authority and was unable to keep order in his kingdom. A period of anarchy replaced one of peaceful prosperity.

In the neighbouring state of Borduria the people observed Syldavia's decline, and their king profited by this opportunity to invade the country. Borduria annexed Syldavia in 1195.

For almost a century Syldavia groaned under the foreign yoke. In 1275 Baron Almaszout repeated the exploits of Hveghi by coming down from the hills and routing the Bordurians in less than six months.

He was proclaimed King in 1277, taking the name of Ottokar. He was, however, much less powerful than Muskar.

The barons who had helped him in the campaign against the Bordurians forced him to grant them a charter, based on the English Magna Carta signed by King John (Lackland). This marked the beginning of the feudal system in Syldavia.

Ottokar I of Syldavia should not be confused with the Ottakars (Premysls) who were Dukes, and later Kings, of Bohemia.

This period was noteworthy for the rise in power of the nobles, who fortified their castles and maintained bands of armed mercenaries, strong enough to oppose the King's forces.

But the true founder of the kingdom of Syldavia was Ottokar IV, who ascended the throne in 1370.

From the time of his accession he initiated widespread reforms. He raised a powerful army and subdued the arrogant nobles, confiscating their wealth.

He fostered the advancement of the arts, of letters, commerce and agriculture.

He united the whole nation and gave it that security, both at home and abroad, so necessary for the renewal of prosperity.

It was he who pronounced those famous words: '*Eih bennek, eih blavek*', which have become the motto of Syldavia.

The origin of this saying is as follows:

One day Baron Staszrvich, son of one of the dispossessed nobles whose lands had been forfeited to the crown, came before the sovereign and recklessly claimed the throne of Syldavia.

The King listened in silence, but when the presumptuous baron's speech ended with a demand that he deliver up his sceptre, the King rose and cried fiercely: 'Come and get it!'

Mad with rage, the young baron drew his sword, and before the retainers could intervene, fell upon the King.

The King stepped swiftly aside, and as his adversary passed him, carried forward by the impetus of his charge, Ottokar struck

Well, that's all very interesting, but . . .

. . . I must be on my guard. Without his glasses this man can pick out a flock of sheep from as high up as this. He has good eyes for a short-sighted person! . . . And another strange thing: ever since I found him packing his bags I haven't seen him smoke a single cigarette.

. . . Unless I'm very much mistaken, I'm travelling with an impostor! . . . If that's so, then everything fits in . . . The shouts I heard on the telephone were from the real Professor Alembick. He has been kidnapped and this man has taken his place.

He must be exposed! At Prague I'll pull off that false beard, and have him arrested!

Prague? . . . Already?

Yes, we are landing . . .

Now's my chance!

OH!

OUCH!

?

I . . . I'm sorry . . . I . . . I missed a step . . . I beg your pardon . . .

D-don't mention it! . . .

Professor Alembick? . . . Your special plane is waiting.

It's a real beard!

But what about his glasses? . . . Not that that proves anything. Plenty of people can see better at a distance than near to . . . As for the cigarettes, perhaps he has simply given up smoking . . .

You see, Snowy, in rough weather when the plane bumps about you fasten yourself into the seat like this . . .

There is the frontier . . . We are now over Syldavia . . .

What lovely country . . .

Very pretty, isn't it? I'll let you admire it a bit more closely . . .

There! . . . Happy landings! . . .

TINTIN?!

! ?

Quick, the parachute! . . .

No time to buckle it on! . . .

Mind the jerk when it opens! . . .

23

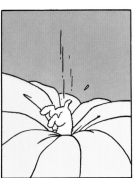

Zrälükz! . . .
Wooah!

Czesztot on klebcz!

Splendid! . . . Snowy fell into the parachute . . . He's safe!

My aeroplane . . . BRRRR . . . I fell . . . Crash! . . . Into the straw . . .

Czestot wzryzkar nietz on vaghabontz! . . . Czestot bätczer yhzer kzömmetz noh dascz politzski? . . . .

Snowy! Snowy!

Wooah! Wooah!

Kzommet micz omhz, noh dascz politzski!

Come with you to the police? . . . With pleasurski! . . . I've got a complaint to make!

ГЕНДАРМАСКАИА

Captain, what I have to say is of the utmost importance . . . May I speak to you in private? . . .

Er . . . Yes . . . Leave us alone . . .

First, may I ask you a question? . . . I read in a brochure about Syldavia that if your King loses his sceptre he will be forced to abdicate. Is that true? . . .

As a matter of fact it is . . . But how does this concern you?

I'll tell you. I am certain there's a conspiracy against King Muskar XII, and that certain people will try to steal the sceptre from him!

What's that you say? . . . What makes you imagine such a thing?

I'll explain . . . But first, are you sure we are not overheard?

Definitely not. Go on . . .

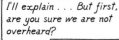

This must be serious. They've been in there nearly an hour . . .

You have just rendered a great service to my country: I thank you. I will telegraph at once to Klow and have Professor Alembick arrested. I'm sure I can rely on you for absolute secrecy . . .

Of course . . . But I must be on my way . . . Can I hire a car?

There isn't a single car in the village. But tomorrow is market-day in Klow. You can go with a peasant who is leaving here today. But you won't arrive there until morning . . .

Too bad, but I have no choice. I'll go with the peasant.

Hello? . . . Yes, this is Klow 3324 . . . Yes, Central Committee . . . Trovik speaking . . . Oh it's you Wizskitotz . . . What? . . . Tintin? . . . But that's impossible: the pilot has just told me . . . What? . . . Into some straw! . . . Szplug! He must be prevented from reaching Klow at all costs! . . . Do it how you like . . . Yes, ring up Sirov . . .

Hello? . . . Yes, this is Sirov . . . Hello Wizskitotz . . . Yes . . . A young boy, on the road to Klow . . . In a peasant's cart . . . Good, we'll be waiting in the forest . . . Yes, we'll leave at once . . . Goodbye! . . .

Look out! . . . Here they come! . . .

Hands up! . . .

?

Where's the young foreigner you are taking to Klow? . . .

Th-th-the young f-f-f-foreigner . . .

That's enough! . . . We know he's with you! . . . Search the cart, Zlop!

Th-th-the f-f-foreign . . . er who . . . who w-w-w . . .

Was w-w-w-with m-m-me? . . .

What makes you stutter like that? . . . Fear?

N-n-no! . . . It . . . it . . . it . . . it's b-b-be-because . . . I . . . I . . . I t-t-talk . . . talk . . . talk . . .

Sirov! There's no one there!

!

Szplug! Where can he be? . . . Come on, are you going to talk? . . .

I . . . I . . . w-was g-g-going t-t-to t-tell y-y-you, b-b-but y-y-you in-in-inter-inter-interrupted m-m-me! . . . He st-st-stopped at . . . at . . . at . . . th-th-the Co-co-co-

Cocoa! . . . Cocoa! . . . What cocoa? . . . Have you been drinking? . . .

The Co-Co-Coach-Coachman's Rest, an-an-and . . .

Why didn't you say so sooner?

Quiet! . . . I can hear a car!

An-an-and he . . . he . . . he . . . g-g-g-

If you say one word, or make one move . . . just remember our rifles are trained on you! . . .

L-l-l-listen . . . I . . . I . . . I'm I'm . . .

It's gone . . . We can go back . . .

I . . . I'm t-t-try-trying to t-t-tell . . . yy-yy-yyou . . . th-th-the y-y-young f-f-for-foreigner w-w-

Szplitz on Szplug! Where is he? . . .

W-w-was in . . . in . . . in th-th-that c-c-car w-w-w-which j-j-just papa-papa-passed! . . .

! !

Yes, I am singing tonight at the Winter Garden in Klow . . . Would you like to hear me now? . . .

I'd love to.

Ah, ♫ my beauty ♪ past compare: these jewels ♫ bright I wear! . . .

Was I ever ♪♪ ♩ Margar-i-i-ta? ♪

It's lucky the windows are strong!

Hello? . . . Yes, this is Wizskitotz . . . Ah, it's you Sirov . . . Well? . . . What? . . . Szplug! . . . So it's not your fault? . . . Perhaps you think it's mine, eh? . . . What? . . . If he hadn't stuttered so? . . . If! . . . If! . . . You can get round anything with 'if' . . . I'll telephone to the Chief of Police at Zlip . . . Yes, he's one of us . . . He'll stop him on the road.

Well, how did you like that? . . .

V-very much indeed! . . .

In that case, just to please you I'll sing something else!

!!

Where is the boy who is travelling with you? . . .

He got out earlier on. He'd forgotten something at the Coachman's Rest, so he went back . . .

I would have given any excuse to escape!

Meanwhile, in Klow . . .

So, you wish to have access to the Treasure House to examine the national archives? . . . I won't conceal from you that this is a privilege rarely accorded to a foreigner, but since our ambassador has vouched for you, I think His Majesty will look favourably upon your request.

That's him . . . We'll ask for his papers . . .

Your papers are not in order! . . . Come with us to the police station!

Quite correct: your papers are not in order! . . . I shall have to keep you here until I receive instructions.

But Captain, there must be some mistake! . . . My passport was stamped before I left and . . .

I am sorry, but I cannot allow you to proceed. Take him away!

Captain! . . . You must listen! . . . I have something important to tell you! . . . I . . .

Hello? . . . Wizskitotz? . . . This is Szplodj . . . I've got our fine bird! . . . Yes, we simply picked him up . . . Now what do you want us to do with him? . . . Yes . . . Yes . . . He obviously mustn't get to Klow . . . I'll think it over . . . That's it, ring up in the morning . . . Goodbye . . .

While I cool my heels here, goodness knows what's going on in Klow . . .

Aaaouaaah! . . . It's getting dark . . . I'd better try and get some sleep, as there's nothing else to do . . .

This is Radio Klow . . . We are now broadcasting a concert from the Winter Garden at Klow. The soloist is Signora Bianca Castafiore of La Scala, Milan.

Ah, my beauty ♪ past compare; these jewels bright I wear! ♪ ♪ Was I ever Margarita?

Is it I? ♪ Come reply! ♪ Mirror, mirror tell me truly! ♪♪♪

Next day . . .

This document bearing the royal signature will admit you to the Treasure Chamber. Lieutenant Kromir will escort you there . . .

The regalia is housed in the keep of Kropow Castle. A special guard is mounted over it.

In the name of the King!

Professor, please come with me.

The regalia seems well guarded!

It is! The man who is clever enough to steal it hasn't been born!

There is His Majesty's regalia, Professor! . . .

And this is the Muniments Room, which adjoins the Treasure Chamber. You must forgive me, but two guards will remain with you for as long as you are here. The doors will also be locked from the outside. Those are the orders. I hope you will not be offended.

Not in the least . . .

Meanwhile . . .

You are to take this young man to Klow. But be careful! . . . He is a dangerous ruffian who has been meddling in State secrets . . . In fact, I've been given to understand, on high authority, that it'd be a good thing if he never arrived in   Klow.

These are your orders . . . You, as the driver, will stage a breakdown. You will get out to look at the engine, and the others will follow . . . The prisoner will then try to escape and . . . You understand me?

Yes, sir! . . . But what if he doesn't try to get away?

Don't worry! . . . He will! . . .

I wonder who can have sent me this? . . . A friend? . . . What friend?

BEWARE! YOU ARE GOING TO BE TAKEN TO KLOW TO BE SHOT! YOU MUST TRY TO ESCAPE. ON THE JOURNEY, PRETEND TO BE ASLEEP. THE DRIVER, WHO IS A FRIEND, WILL STAGE A BREAKDOWN AND CALL THE OTHER GUARDS AWAY. THAT WILL BE THE MOMENT FOR YOU TO MAKE YOUR ESCAPE.

A FRIEND

We'd better get rid of this, in case I'm searched.

Here, Snowy, swallow this paper pellet for me . . .

Hurry up now, Snowy, I think someone is coming for us . . .

I suppose you think it's easy?

Why have you stopped? . . .

It's the engine . . .

Let's have a look . . . Oh, it's all right: he's asleep . . .

Look out, he's moving! . . . He's getting out . . . Get ready . . .

A trap! . . . I'm done for!

There he goes! . . . Don't miss! . . .

There's only one way: a nose-dive! . . . Whoops!

BANG
BANG
BANG

WHIZZ

BANG

WHIZZZ

CRACK

It's no good, hold your fire! . . . He's disappeared behind the boulders! . . . He must have broken his neck . . . but we'd better look for him . . .

He fell down there . . . Somewhere behind those rocks . . .

They're coming! . . .

Careful! About here . . .

Szplug! Where is he? We've simply got to find him . . . The captain will never forgive us if we let him get away, after he'd planned that trap . . .

Come on, let's have another look. He can't be far away . . .

Whew! . . . They've passed us . . .

Now, off we go to Klow! . . .

I must watch my step! . . . I see that no one can be trusted! . . . I must warn the King himself.

Meanwhile in Klow . . .

I wonder if I might be permitted to photograph some of the documents?

As a rule that is not allowed, but His Majesty might consent . . .

Ah! Here's the main road again.

Golly, I'm hungry . . .

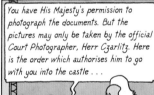

You have His Majesty's permission to photograph the documents. But the pictures may only be taken by the official Court Photographer, Herr Czarlitz. Here is the order which authorises him to go with you into the castle . . .

Klow at last! . . .

When are we going to eat?

Which way to the palace, please?

Follow this street to Ottokar Square, then turn left . . .

DANGER HIGH VOLTAGE

What a downpour! We'll shelter until this is over . . .

Is this a restaurant?

It's stopping now . . .

Come on Snowy! . . . We must hurry to warn the King of the danger he's in . . .

Hurry up, Snowy! Hey, where is Snowy?

Snowy! . . . Snowy! . . . Snowy! . . .

They have wonderful bones in this country, Tintin! . . .

DIPLODOCUS GIGANTICUS

You take that bone back where you found it, at once! You understand... And be quick!...

Ah! There's the palace!

Could His Majesty grant me an audience?... I have most important and urgent business...

Please wait here: I will see if His Majesty's aide-de-camp will see you. Whom shall I announce?...

Tintin.

Mr Tintin?... On important business?... All right, show him in.

Certainly, Signora.... Yes.... yes ... tonight, at half past eight... His Majesty will be delighted... Your servant, Signora...

Meanwhile...

So that's all arranged, Herr Czarlitz... I will come and fetch you in the morning at about nine, and we will go to Kropow Castle together...

Very good, Professor.

So you want an audience with His Majesty? . . . May I ask why? . . .

Er . . . I . . . you must excuse me, but . . . it is highly confidential . . .

Sir, I am His Majesty's aide-de-camp! . . . I venture to say that my sovereign places complete trust in me!

I do not doubt it, Colonel! . . . But the news I have to communicate to the King is so serious that it is for his ears alone.

Very well, I will not insist . . . Will you come back tonight, at about half past eight? I will try and arrange for His Majesty to allow you a few minutes, before his reception at the palace . . .

Thank you very much.

Now for a meal, Snowy!

Hello? . . . Yes, this is the Central Committee. Ah, it's you, Boris. What's the latest news? . . . Yes . . . What? . . . Tintin? . . . Are you sure? But the Chief of Police at Zlip has just sworn that . . . Yes . . . Terribly important information.

But he didn't say what it was? . . . Good! . . . Aha! . . . He'll be back tonight at eight-thirty? . . . That's fine, it gives us time . . . Listen, he must not speak to the King . . . Definitely not! . . . This is what we'll do: listen . . .

That evening . . .

The King is willing to grant you a short interview. Please go with the Captain of the Guard and he will take you to the Audience Chamber. His Majesty will see you there.

Thank you.

Ssh! . . . Here they come . . .

Wooah! Wooah!

?

That mongrel has given us away! . . . Come on! . . .

An ambush! . . .

Got you, my friend. Don't try to resist! . . .

!

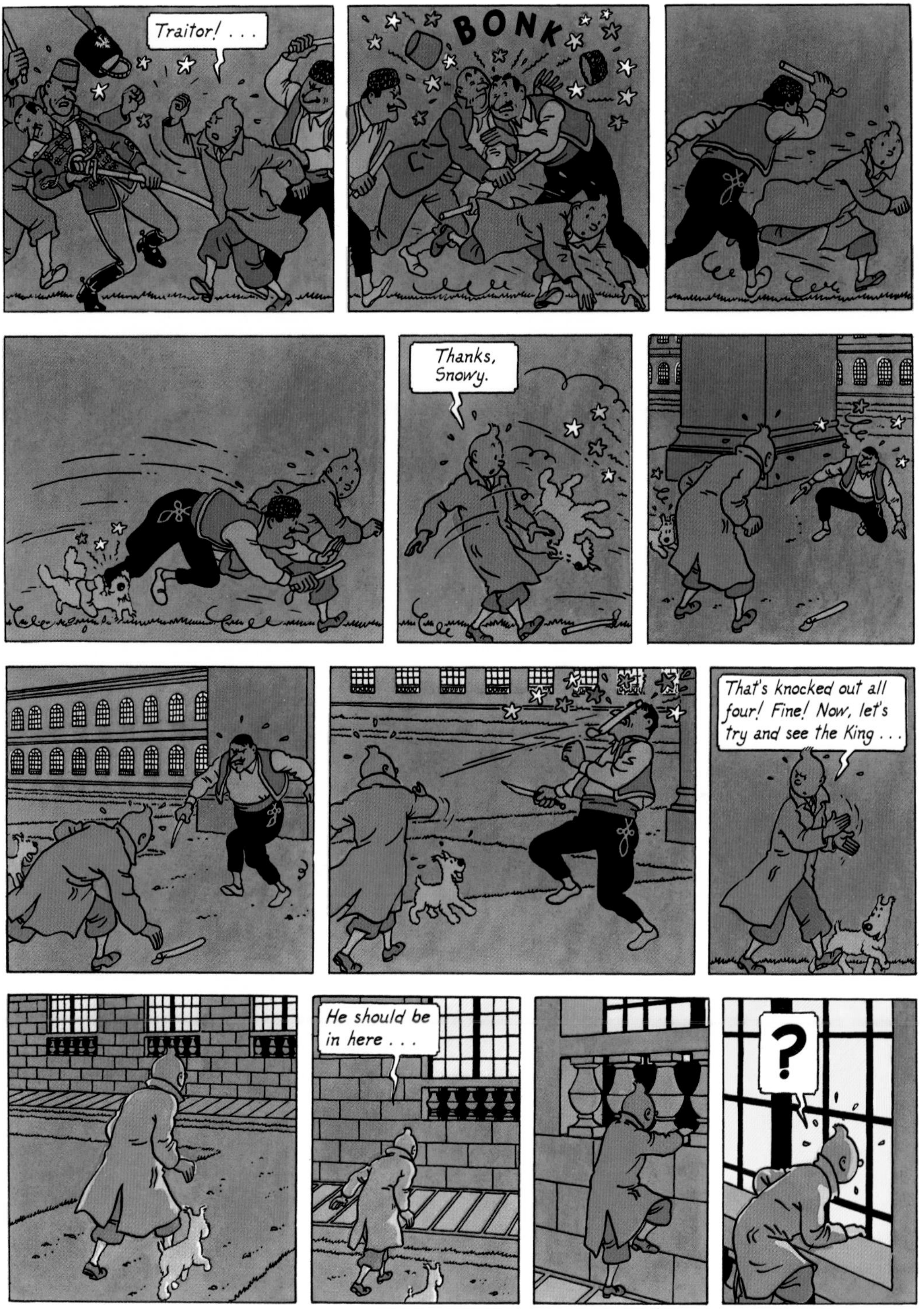
Traitor! . . .
BONK
Thanks, Snowy.
That's knocked out all four! Fine! Now, let's try and see the King . . .
He should be in here . . .
?

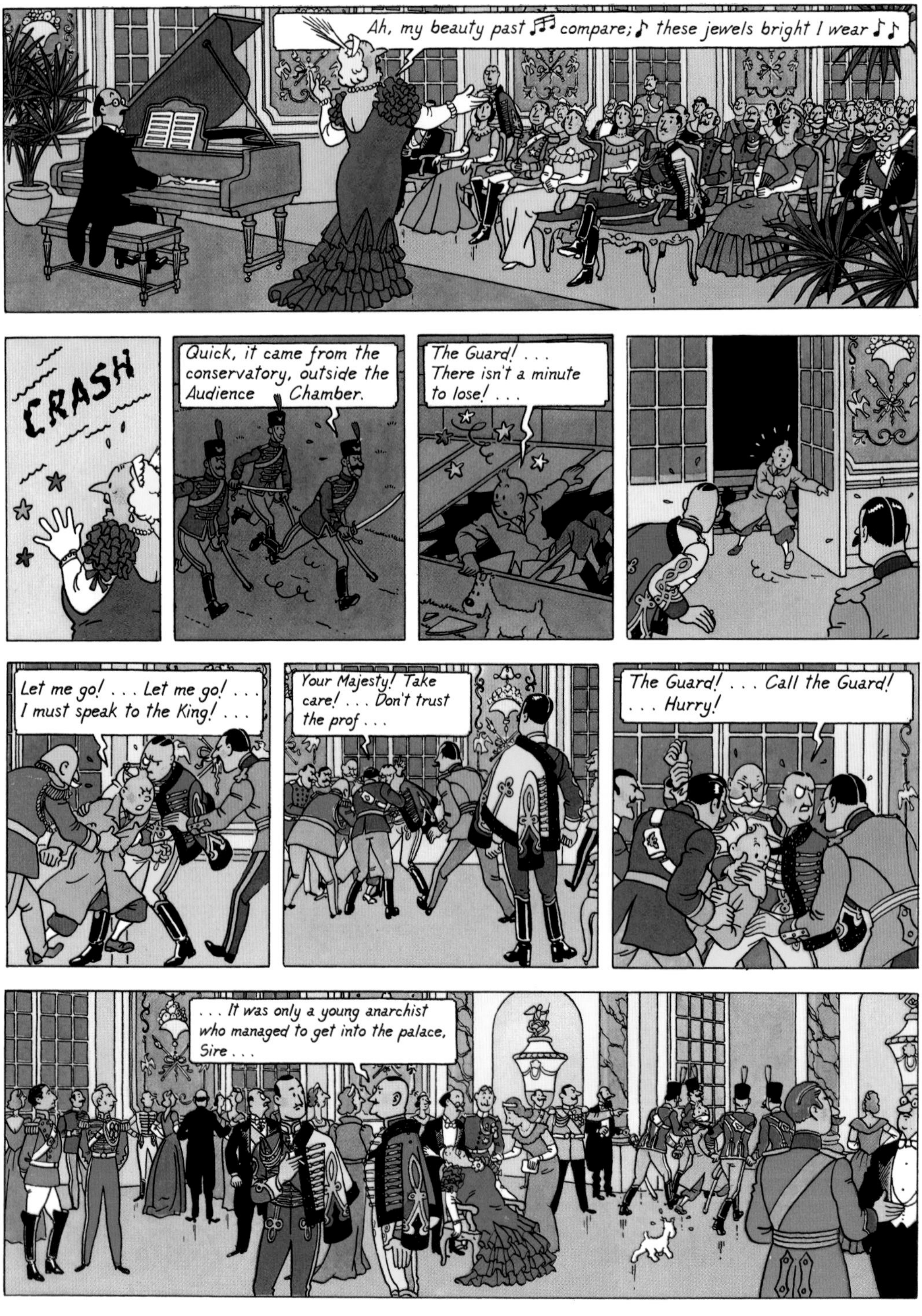
Ah, my beauty past ♫ compare; ♪ these jewels bright I wear ♪♪
CRASH
Quick, it came from the conservatory, outside the Audience Chamber.
The Guard! . . . There isn't a minute to lose! . . .
Let me go! . . . Let me go! . . . I must speak to the King! . . .
Your Majesty! Take care! . . . Don't trust the prof . . .
The Guard! . . . Call the Guard! . . . Hurry!
. . . It was only a young anarchist who managed to get into the palace, Sire . . .

Next morning . . .

More time wasted! . . . And I'm sure the conspirators won't be wasting theirs! . . .

CLINK CLINK CLINK

You are being transferred to the State Prison to await trial. Come with us. The police van is outside . . .

Hello, this is St. Vladimir's Hospital . . . An accident? . . . Casualties? In Moltus Street? . . . All right, I'll send an ambulance.

This one still hasn't come round . . .

Yes, definitely suffering from concussion . . .

We'd better go back for the others . . .

A very useful thing, concussion . . . Come on, Snowy! Now or never . . .

Aha! That's done the trick! . . . Now back to the palace!

I must see the King at all costs.

This time nothing is going to stop me speaking to him! . . .

You aren't hurt, I hope?

No, thank you. I'm all right . . . Great snakes! . . . The King!

Take care, Sire! . . . This is the young anarchist who tried . . .

?

Don't shoot, Sir! . . . Please listen! . . . I am not an anarchist. I wanted to warn you . . . Even at this moment those scoundrels may be trying to steal your sceptre!

What do you mean?

It's the truth, Sir. I am certain that Professor Alembick is an impostor. Coming to Syldavia to study the archives was only a blind. He and his accomplices plan to steal King Ottokar's sceptre, and so force you to give up your throne!

By Vladimir! Can it be?

Meanwhile . . .

And this man is in with them, Sir . . . That is why he tried to stop me speaking to you! . . .

He's in the plot too?

It's a lie, Sire!

He is lying, Sire, and I will . . .

You will return to the palace at once and await my orders! . . . I myself will go to Kropow Castle with this young man and prove for myself the truth of his allegations! . . .

We must hurry, Sir . . . I'm sure there's not a moment to lose . . .

That's that . . . May we now go into the Treasure Chamber, and photograph the crown and sceptre? . . .

Certainly.

40

The light is not very good. We'll have to use a flash-bulb . . .

We're nearly there . . . Those are the towers of Kropow Castle . . . the sceptre is in the keep, that square tower in the centre . . . I only hope we're not too late! . . .

The King! . . .

Everything seems quite normal . . . We are in time!

I hope so, Sir . . .

Where is Professor Alembick?

In the Treasure Chamber, Sire, with the Governor of the Castle and Herr Czarlitz . . .

Open up! In the name of the King!

No answer! Quick, bring me the other keys!

Could it really be possible?

Let us hope not, Sir . . . Ah! Here is the guard with the keys.

Panel 1:

Next morning . . .

So, Lord Chamberlain, the sceptre has not been recovered yet? . . .

Alas no, Sire . . . But I have secured the services of two detectives of international repute. I expect them any minute now . . .

Panel 2:

THUD

What's going on? . . . Go and see.

Ah, I think I know who they are.

Panel 3:

?

Er . . . We are the detectives who . . . Hm . . . We . . . we slipped . . . and . . .

Yes . . . and we fell down . . .

Panel 4:

Sire, may I present Mr Thomson and Mr Thompson, certified detectives . . .

Welcome to Syldavia, gentlemen . . .

Majesty, your sire is very good . . . Good Majesty . . . no, I mean . . .

To be precise . . . it's a majesty, Your Pleasure . . .

Panel 5:

We thank you for answering our call so promptly, and for placing your experience at the service of the Crown . . . This is Mr Tintin, who will give you all the details of this business . . .

Tintin! Well I never!

Panel 6:

This is the position . . . Someone has stolen the King's sceptre! . . . When His Majesty and I entered the Treasure Chamber we found the Governor of the Castle, two of his men, the photographer Czarlitz, and Professor Alembick, whom you know. All of them were in a coma, and none of the five came to until this morning . . .

Have they been questioned? . . .

Panel 7:

Yes, and their statements agree on all points. Herr Czarlitz decided to use a flash-bulb. After the flash the room filled with thick smoke. They began to choke, and then passed out . . .

Good. But . . . hm . . . did anyone think of searching these people? . . .

Panel 8:

Of course! Even the guards' halberds were taken to pieces, and the camera tripod, to make sure the sceptre wasn't hidden there. They tapped every inch of the room looking for a secret passage, but found nothing! The only door through which the thief could escape was guarded by two sentries, who saw no one leave . . .

Panel 9:

Your Majesty, this is all childishly simple! . . . With your permission we will go to Kropow Castle and demonstrate how your sceptre was stolen . . .

Panel 10:

Very well, we'll go! . . .

Goodness, they're smarter than I thought!

Panel 11:

Be careful: the marble is very slippery . . .

This is the Treasure Chamber. The sceptre was here . . .

As we said, Your Majesty: the whole thing is childishly simple!

This is what happened. One of the five people present was in the plot. He collapsed when the smoke was released, but took care to hold a handkerchief to his nose. When he was sure the others had been put to sleep he got up, opened the glass case, seized the sceptre, opened the window and dropped the sceptre into the courtyard. There an accomplice collected it, took it away, and that was that!

Impossible, gentlemen! The courtyard is guarded. No one goes there but the sentries; and the sentries are above suspicion . . . They are men of absolute trust who would die rather than betray their King!

As a matter of fact the guard patrolling this side of the tower did hear a window open and shut. But he did not notice anything unusual . . .

Exactly! . . . Because the thief must have thrown the sceptre over the ramparts surrounding the castle! . . . An accomplice waited there, picked it up, and made off.

However, you shall see . . . Could you get me something the same size as the sceptre? . . .

Certainly . . .

But look! It is at least a hundred yards from this window to the ramparts! . . . And there are bars . . .

What do they matter? . . . It just needs a good aim . . .

There . . . Will this do? . . .

Perfectly.

Now I'll show you . . .

? BONG

Clumsy oaf! . . . Let me show you the right way to do it! . . .

Watch carefully! . . .

BONG

?

You can see for yourselves that the sceptre didn't leave this room like that! . . .

Yes . . . Yes . . . maybe. Anyway, we'd like to question Alembick and Czarlitz . . .

Sire! . . . Sire! . . . Ah, at last I've found you . . .

?

Sire! . . . It's unbelievable! . . . Professor Alembick and Herr Czarlitz . . .

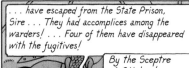
. . . have escaped from the State Prison, Sire . . . They had accomplices among the warders! . . . Four of them have disappeared with the fugitives!

By the Sceptre of Ottokar!

Accomplices! . . . Accomplices! . . . They are everywhere! . . . Oh, this plot was well laid: all is lost!

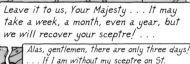
Leave it to us, Your Majesty . . . It may take a week, a month, even a year, but we will recover your sceptre! . . .

Alas, gentlemen, there are only three days! . . . If I am without my sceptre on St. Vladimir's Day, I have no choice but to abdicate!

'Only three days', said Columbus, 'and I will give you a new world!' Only three days, Majesty, and we swear to bring your sceptre, bound hand and foot . . .

Thank you, gentlemen! May you succeed.

This time our honour is at stake! We have sworn to find the sceptre; we must keep our word!

To be precise: we must keep our word!

St. Vladimir protect them! . . . They will succeed, won't they? . . .

I hope so, Sir, with all my heart!

In any case, I'd like your permission to try to solve this mystery myself.

Thank you, my friend. Whatever happens, I shall never forget what you have done for me!

The vital thing is to find out HOW the sceptre was stolen . . .

TO

YS

⁉ ⚡!

Eureka! . . . Eureka! . . . I've got it!

YS

Quick, back to the castle!

I've got it! . . . Come with me to the Treasure Chamber! . . . I'll show you! . . .

Show me what?

How the sceptre was stolen! . . . Quick! Follow me!

Don't go so fast! . . . Wait for me! . . .

Has he gone in? . . .

Yes, sir . . .

? OW!

?! ?

What happened? . . . Quick, tell us! . . .

The camera! . . . Look at the camera! . . .

A spring? . . .

Yes, this spring came out. It hit me in the face and knocked me out! . . .

It's amazing! . . . How did you discover that?

By walking past a toy-shop! . . . I saw a little spring gun; it gave me the idea that perhaps the camera was faked up to hide a spring capable of throwing the sceptre beyond the castle ramparts! And my guess was right! . . .

Watch! . . . There's the spring back in place . . . I insert into the tube this stick used by the two detectives . . .

I place the camera by the window, the forked end of our makeshift sceptre through the bars . . .

I click the shutter, and . . . Whoops!

It's fallen in the wood, beyond the river! . . . I'm going to have a look round over there.

You will find a boat down by the bank . . .

?

If that fool Czarlitz had aimed at the clump of birch trees by the river bank as we agreed, we'd have found the sceptre long ago . . .

So they haven't found it yet! . . . There's not a moment to lose! . . . I must get back, and have this wood surrounded.

HOORAY! . . .

Hooray! I've found it!

Now, I must give the others the slip . . .

Crumbs! They've got me!

Yes, got you all right!

The sceptre, Snowy! . . . Save the sceptre! . . .

Come here, you mangy cur! . . . Come here!

Here's the river! . . . In we go! . . . Just let them try and catch me!

?

!

BANG
BANG

Every man for himself, boys! . . . The police! . . .

Poor old Tintin!

Where's the sceptre?

They've got it again! . . . Snowy dropped it!

Too late!

How did you know I was here?

When we went back to the castle they told us you had crossed the river . . .

There's the King . . . They told him, too. He went round by the bridge while we crossed in a boat . . .

Well, what has happened? . . .

Those gangsters have got away in a car, with the sceptre! . . . If you will lend us your car, Sir, we three will try and catch them . . .

They haven't got much of a start on us . . . We'll soon catch them up.

We're almost out of petrol . . . We'll have to stop at the first pump we come to . . .

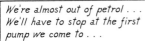

Ah! There's one . . .

. . Five gallons! . . . And make it snappy! . . .

Another twenty miles to the frontier . . . Good! . . . In half an hour we shall be clear of Syldavia, and the sceptre will be safe!

The King's car! . . . They're after us!

We certainly caught them on the hop!
. . . They've taken to the mountains!

They hadn't even time to
get back into their car . . .

We must hurry! . . .
They mustn't get away!

They're still following
us . . .

We must stop this! . . .
We'll fool them! . . .

Come on! . . .
We'll get them! . . .

BANG

Take cover everybody . . .
They are shooting at us!

BANG

Where have Thomson and
Thompson got to? . . . I
can't see them anywhere.

BANG

CRACK

There must be some way
of catching them . . .

Follow me, Snowy, and don't
show yourself! . . . We'll sneak
round behind them.

Hello, where's the third one? . . .

Not a sign of life . . .

Perhaps we hit him . . . Look! There are the other two . . .

Hands up!

Now, I see! . . . You blocked our way while your pal got away with the sceptre! . . .

Quick! You look after these thugs! . . . I'm going on . . .

Szplug! I can't understand it . . . He's still on my tail! . . .

It's getting dark . . . We can't keep this up much longer.

We can't go on now . . . We'll have to spend the night here! . . .

We can only wait until it's light . . .

Next day, at dawn . . .

Off we go Snowy! . . . We simply must recover the sceptre!

We'll walk fast: That will warm us up . . .

SYLDAVIA · BORDURIA

The frontier at last!
. . . I'm safe! . . .

SYLDAVIA · BOR

SYLDAVIA

Another yard and he'd
have been over . . . !

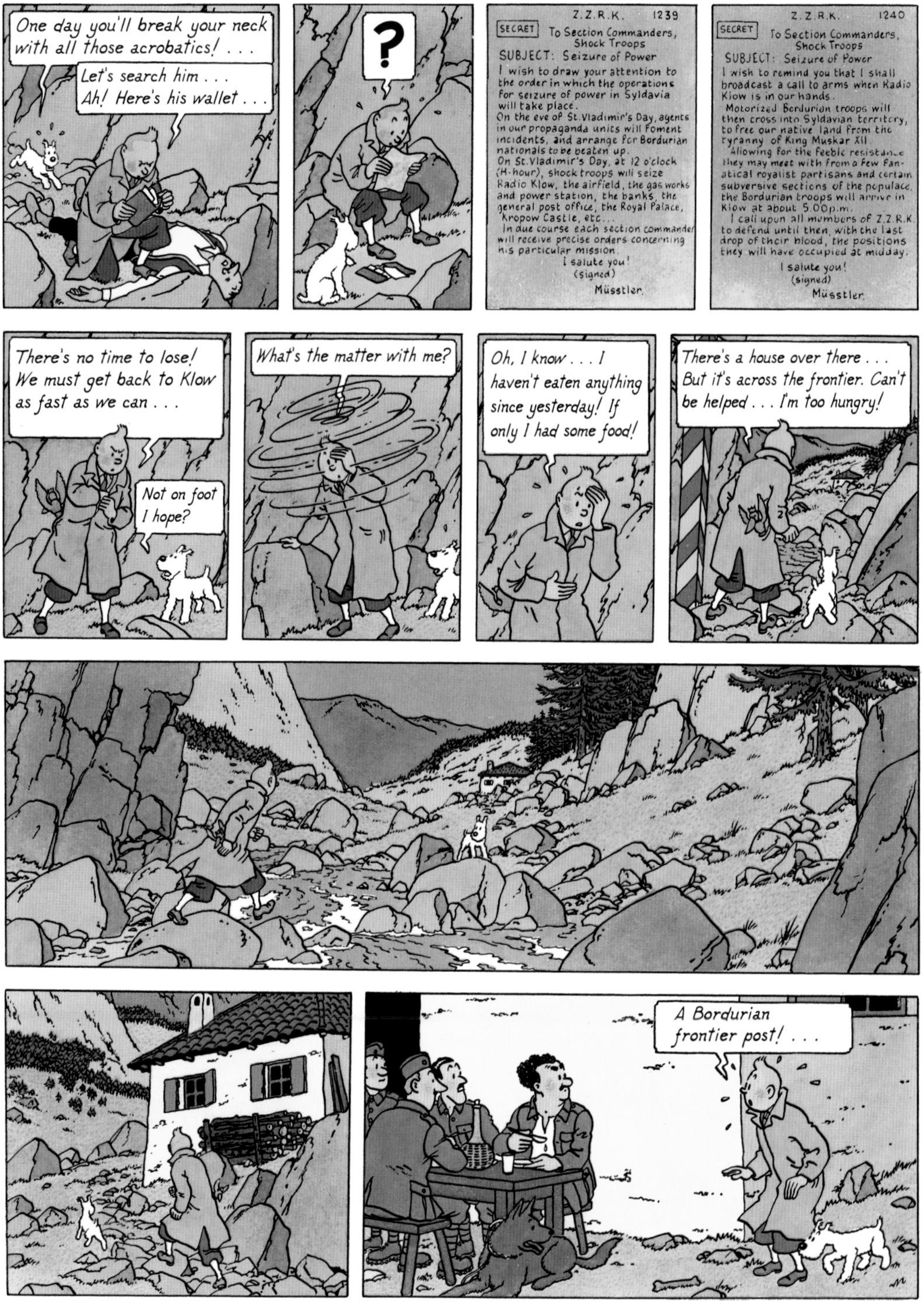
One day you'll break your neck with all those acrobatics! . . .
Let's search him . . . Ah! Here's his wallet . . .
?
Z.Z.R.K. 1239
SECRET
To Section Commanders, Shock Troops
SUBJECT: Seizure of Power
I wish to draw your attention to the order in which the operations for seizure of power in Syldavia will take place.
On the eve of St. Vladimir's Day, agents in our propaganda units will foment incidents, and arrange for Bordurian nationals to be beaten up.
On St. Vladimir's Day, at 12 o'clock (H-hour), shock troops will seize Radio Klow, the airfield, the gas works and power station, the banks, the general post office, the Royal Palace, Kropow Castle, etc . . .
In due course each section commander will receive precise orders concerning his particular mission.
I salute you!
(signed)
Müsstler.
Z.Z.R.K. 1240
SECRET
To Section Commanders, Shock Troops
SUBJECT: Seizure of Power
I wish to remind you that I shall broadcast a call to arms when Radio Klow is in our hands.
Motorized Bordurian troops will then cross into Syldavian territory, to free our native land from the tyranny of King Muskar XII.
Allowing for the feeble resistance they may meet with from a few fanatical royalist partisans and certain subversive sections of the populace, the Bordurian troops will arrive in Klow at about 5.00p.m.
I call upon all members of Z.Z.R.K. to defend until then, with the last drop of their blood, the positions they will have occupied at midday.
I salute you!
(signed)
Müsstler.
There's no time to lose! We must get back to Klow as fast as we can . . .
Not on foot I hope?
What's the matter with me?
Oh, I know . . . I haven't eaten anything since yesterday! If only I had some food!
There's a house over there . . . But it's across the frontier. Can't be helped . . . I'm too hungry!
A Bordurian frontier post! . . .

Crumbs! He's come to . . .
I'm cut off!

BANG

WOOF
WOOF

He's a dangerous Syldavian spy!
. . . We must capture him! . . .

Look out! He may
be hiding in that
house . . .

No, he's gone
. . . Come on!

What's the matter with him?
SNIFF

What's he
sniffing at? . . .
SNIFF
SNIFF
SNIFF

Pep . . . Tchoo! . . .
It's pepper . . . Aaaa
. . . tchoo!

Little devil! He's scattered
pepper to put the dog off
the scent!

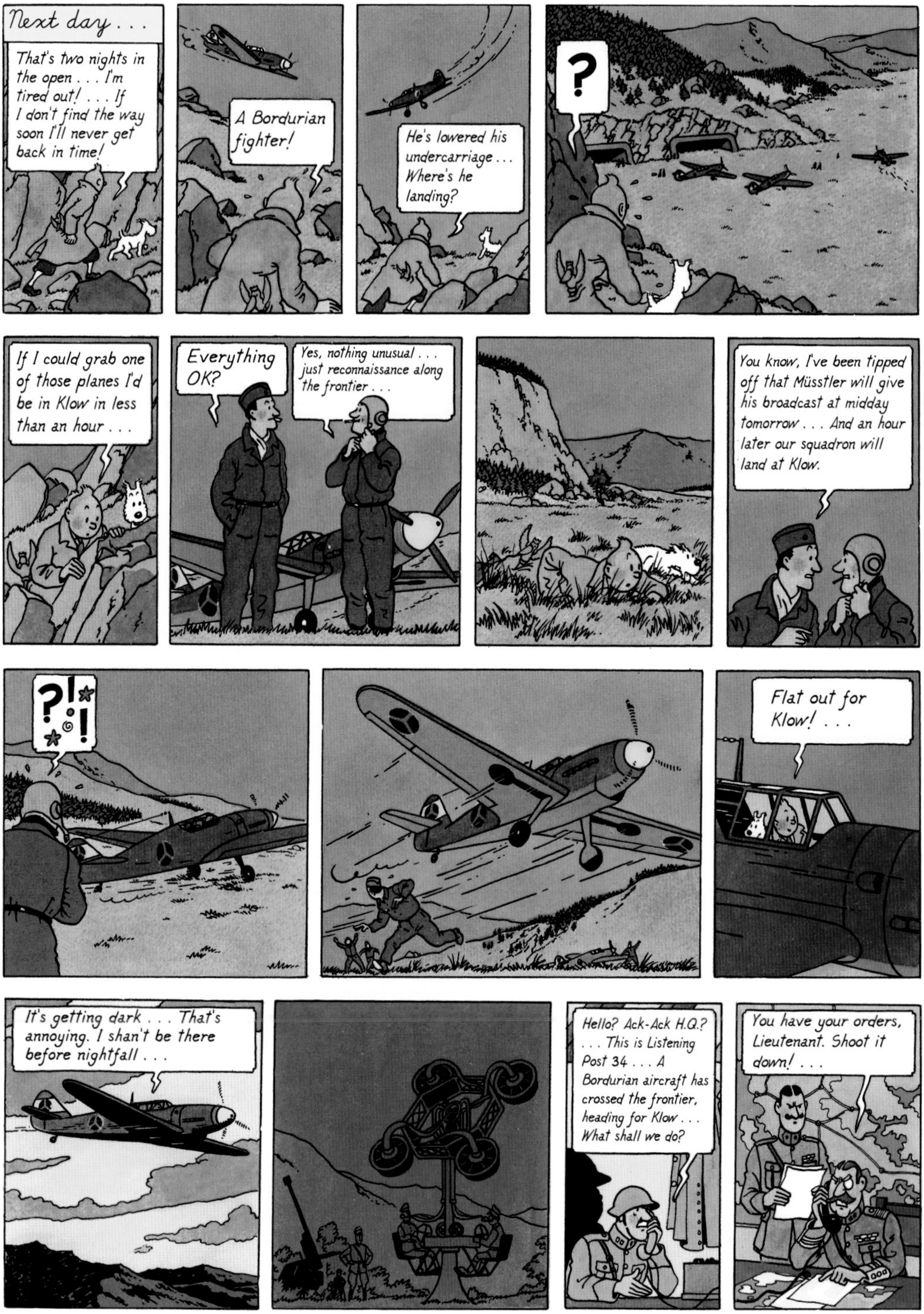
Next day . . .
That's two nights in the open . . . I'm tired out! . . . If I don't find the way soon I'll never get back in time!
A Bordurian fighter!
He's lowered his undercarriage . . . Where's he landing?
?
If I could grab one of those planes I'd be in Klow in less than an hour . . .
Everything OK?
Yes, nothing unusual . . . just reconnaissance along the frontier . . .
You know, I've been tipped off that Müsstler will give his broadcast at midday tomorrow . . . And an hour later our squadron will land at Klow.
?!!
Flat out for Klow! . . .
It's getting dark . . . That's annoying. I shan't be there before nightfall . . .
Hello? Ack-Ack H.Q.? . . . This is Listening Post 34 . . . A Bordurian aircraft has crossed the frontier, heading for Klow . . . What shall we do?
You have your orders, Lieutenant. Shoot it down! . . .

Hello! . . . Searchlights!

They've picked us up! . . .
I hope they . . .

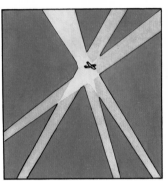

Crumbs! . . . They're firing . . . at me!

Got him! . . . Look,
he's on fire . . .

 Ah, a signpost! . . . That's a stroke of luck!

 ISTOW 19½ miles KLOW 15¾ miles

 Sixteen miles: that's five hours' walk! . . . A mere trifle!

 A farm! . . . Stables! . . . If only I could borrow a horse . . . That's a splendid idea!

 Aha, here's a horse! . . . Whoa there! . . . Good, here's a saddle too . . . Whoa now! Gently does it . . .

 On the whole I think we'd better go on foot. Why not? . . . A little walk will do us good.

 That night . . . Things are grave, Sire! . . . the people are suspicious: there are rumours that the sceptre is missing. Furthermore . . .

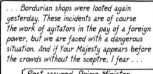
 . . . Bordurian shops were looted again yesterday. These incidents are of course the work of agitators in the pay of a foreign power, but we are faced with a dangerous situation. And if Your Majesty appears before the crowds without the sceptre, I fear . . .

Rest assured, Prime Minister, there will be no bloodshed. I will abdicate.

 No, Sir, you will not abdicate . . . ! TINTIN! ?

 Your Majesty, I have your sceptre with me now! Saved!

 Here it is! . . . I . . . Great snakes! I've lost it on the way!

Lucky I saw the sceptre fall out of his pocket!

!

???

Saved! ... I am saved! ... How happy this makes me!

Saved for the moment only, Sir. I have discovered something else . . .

I found these on the ruffians I went after.

'Seizure of power'! ... And it's signed Müsstler ... Müsstler, the leader of the Iron Guard!

Not a moment to lose! Arrest Müsstler and his associates at once!

Yes, Sire! ...

General, the review of the army will not take place tomorrow as arranged. By 8 a.m., crack regiments will occupy defensive positions along the frontier. And take over all the strategic points which the rebels plan to attack ...

Very good, Sire!

Some hours later . . .

COCKADOODLEDOO

BOOM

BOOM

Guns! ...

Come in!

Oh, it's you! ...What is all that firing for?

That? ...

They are firing a salute for St. Vladimir's Day ... Hurry up and dress, or we shall miss the procession.

And so the royal carriage leaves the palace . . . the King, smiling, bare-headed, is holding the sceptre of Ottokar in his hand . . . A great roar of welcome greets His Majesty, a roar which fades only when the strains of our national anthem swell from a thousand voices . . .

And now the King is once more in his palace. Time and again the delirious crowds have called His Majesty back on to the balcony to receive their tumultuous acclaim. But now he is seated here in the Throne Room, where an investiture is taking place . . .

My Lords, Ladies and Gentlemen. Never in our long history has the Order of the Golden Pelican been conferred upon a foreigner. But today with the full agreement of Our ministers, We bestow this high distinction upon Mr Tintin, to express Our gratitude for the great services he has rendered to Our country . . .

Tintin, Knight of the Order of the Golden Pelican . . .

Hurrah! . . . Hurrah! . . .

Some days later . . .

I expect you will like to hear the result of our enquiries. You already know that Müsstler, leader of the Iron Guard, has been arrested with most of his followers. Calling themselves the Iron Guard they were in fact the Z.Z.R.K., the Zyldav Zentral Revolutzionär Komitzät, whose aims were the deposition of our King, and the annexation of our country by Borduria . . .

Professor Alembick was also arrested at Müsstler's home where he hid after the theft of the sceptre. This little book was found on him . . .

Hassanov, Igor. Ambassador. a very close friend. Met him in Belgrade in 1913 at a sigillographical congress. Gave me a letter of introduction to study national archives in Klow. He

Kavaroutch Syldavian Secret Agent. Keeps an eye on Syldavian organisations abroad. Pretends to be an artist. Suspect. Get rid of him!

I know him. He's the man who collapsed in my room! But look! . . . That's me! . . .

Tintin. Reporter. Brought back my brief-case. Showed him my collection of seals. Mentioned my visit to Zyld-uria. Said I needed a secretary. Promised to send him this book on DON'T TRUST HIM.

It's incredible! . . . But what was this note book for? . . .

So that they would know everyone who went to see the real Professor Alembick . . . Here is another photograph found at Müsstler's house which is the key to the puzzle . . .

MINISTRY OF THE INTERIOR

OFFICE OF THE MINISTER

Twins! . . . I might have guessed it! . . . But what happened to the real professor? . . .

Well, I've just read the London newspapers. Listen: 'During a search carried out yesterday in a house occupied by Syldavian nationals, the police found Professor Alembick, the scholar. He had been imprisoned in a cellar for some weeks. He said he had been kidnapped on the eve of his departure for Syldavia, and his passport was taken . . .'

Now I see it all! First the shouts on the telephone; then the professor not wearing his glasses, and not smoking any more . . . It explains everything.

Meanwhile at Bordurian military headquarters . . .

. . . to prove our peaceful intentions, despite the inexplicable attitude of the Syldavians, I have ordered our troops to withdraw fifteen miles from the frontier . . .

Next day . . .

In a private audience this morning the King received Mr Tintin, Mr Thomson and Mr Thompson, who paid their respects before leaving Syldavia. Afterwards the party left by road for Douma, where they embarked in a flying boat of the regular Douma-Southampton service . . .

RADIO KLOW
SZCHT-SILENCE

Some hours later . . .

Ten past six. We're there . . .

Goodness, what on earth's happening? . . .

We're falling into the sea . . .

We aren't *FALLING*: we're landing! This is a flying-boat, remember!

? ?

How absurd! . . . I had completely forgotten!

Me too! . . . That was a good joke!

Isn't it amazing how absent-minded one can be! . . .

Quite absurd!

I can still hear you shouting: 'We're falling into the sea'!

Ha Ha!
Ha Ha!
Ha Ha!

HERGÉ.

THE REAL-LIFE INSPIRATION BEHIND TINTIN'S ADVENTURES

Written by Stuart Tett
with the collaboration of Studio Moulinsart.

Discover something new and exciting

HERGÉ

Childhood

In *King Ottokar's Sceptre* we catch a glimpse of Hergé's sensitivity toward pompous music. Perhaps the author's aversion to opera can be traced to his childhood? The photo on the left shows Georges Remi in 1912. His mother liked to let his hair grow!

In 1910, when he was three years old, Hergé's parents took him to the World's Fair, a large exhibition being held in Brussels. They were relaxing in the German section of the exhibition when a brass band started playing loud "oompah" music. It was too much for the young child; he kicked and screamed, and there was nothing that could be done. It looks like the future Hergé was forever affected by this tuneful trauma!

Perhaps Captain Haddock's destruction of an orchestra in *The Seven Crystal Balls* is no accident. Was Hergé getting his revenge, many years after the World's Fair?

about Tintin and his creator Hergé!

TINTIN

Anyway, we know his name is Tintin.

Inspiration

Your Young Readers Editions tell you all about the inspiration behind Tintin's adventures, but what about the inspiration behind the character of Tintin himself?

Hergé's first job was working in the office of the newspaper *Le Vingtième Siècle* (meaning "the twentieth century"). He read the news and followed reports written by the French journalist Albert Londres (1884–1932). Londres was one of the founders of investigative journalism, reporting news gleaned from careful, and sometimes undercover, research. His dedication to getting the true inside story led Londres on many adventures, just like Tintin!

Albert Londres

As for Tintin's physical appearance, it is likely that Hergé was inspired by the slim build and blond hair (sometimes styled into a quiff!) of his younger brother, Paul Remi.

Hergé's brother, Paul Remi

THE TRUE STORY
…behind *King Ottokar's Sceptre*

The big question in many people's minds after reading *King Ottokar's Sceptre* is "Where exactly is the country of Syldavia?" Over the next few pages we will try to find out!

> . . . And this is a very unusual seal, which I found quite by chance in Prague. It is the seal of Ottokar IV, King of Syldavia . . .
>
> Oh?. . .

The story begins when Tintin, doing his good deed for the day, returns a lost brief-case to its rightful owner. Professor Alembick invites Tintin in and shows the curious young reporter his collection of antique seals.

Once upon a time…

The use of wax seals—blobs of hot wax stamped with initials or logos—to authenticate documents arose in Europe in around the seventh century. Check out the antique seals below: do any look like the seal of Syldavia?

There are, in fact, thousands of seals, and many look similar. But perhaps there is another clue to the real-life model for Syldavia—in its coat of arms.

Thirteenth-century seal used by Sophie of Thuringia, the Duchess of Brabant.

Thirteenth-century seal used by the canon of a church in Liège, Belgium.

The seal of a real King Ottokar—Ottokar II of Bohemia (1233–1278).

Coat of arms

Hergé created a coat of arms—a type of logo used to represent a country, family, individual or organization—for Syldavia. On this page you can find out more about the design of coats of arms and see some real-life examples of these fascinating symbols, which were first used by knights and rulers in the twelfth century.

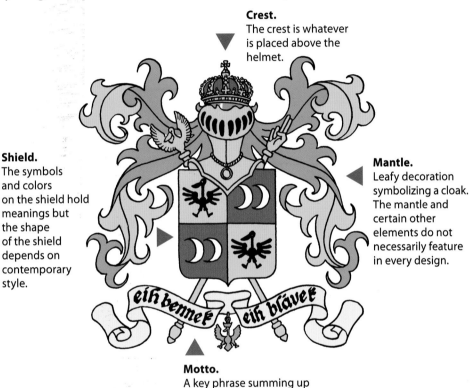

Crest.
The crest is whatever is placed above the helmet.

Shield.
The symbols and colors on the shield hold meanings but the shape of the shield depends on contemporary style.

Mantle.
Leafy decoration symbolizing a cloak. The mantle and certain other elements do not necessarily feature in every design.

Motto.
A key phrase summing up the spirit of the arms-bearer.

The coat of arms of the Dutch municipality of Wassenaar.

The coat of arms of the Swiss town of Hittnau.

A Polish coat of arms dating back to the sixteenth century.

The Belgian coat of arms. The motto means "Strength in Union."

The history of Syldavia

Hergé kindly went so far as to include a full travel brochure in *King Ottokar's Sceptre* (pages 19–21) just so readers could learn about Syldavia. One of the pages of the brochure is an illustration of the twelfth-century battle of Zileheroum, in which the Slavs vanquished the Turks. Hergé based his drawing on real antique paintings called miniatures.

Fifteenth-century miniature from Mongolia.

Once upon a time...

When Hergé wrote about the Turks invading Syldavia in the tenth century, he was mirroring the real-life expansion of the Islamic Ottoman Empire between the fourteenth and sixteenth centuries. But in the end the Ottoman Empire swallowed up dozens of countries...which makes the comparison less useful when trying to pinpoint the location of Syldavia.

Fourteenth-century manuscript

There is one part of the brochure that is not in English: an extract from a manuscript entitled *The Memorable Deeds of Ottokar IV*. Hergé cleverly rearranged words from Brusseleir—the Brussels dialect he knew and had already used in *The Broken Ear* (check out the Young Readers Edition of that story)—to create a medieval Syldavian script. Perhaps this text will give us a clue to the location of Syldavia in Europe? Check out the (very rough) translation below!

"Ottokar, you are a false king, so your throne is mine."
"Really?" said King Ottokar. "Come and get it then!"
Then the king hit Baron Staszrvich on the head. Pathetic Staszrvich bleated, "Oh!" and then the nanny goat fell to the floor.

Well, that wasn't very helpful! As for what King Ottokar IV of Syldavia is saying in the picture, "Eih bennek eih blāvek" translates as "Here I am, here I stay," although the English translators of Tintin changed the motto to "If you gather thistles, expect prickles."

Crash landing

Tintin has just had a lucky escape, landing in a pile of hay when he let go of his parachute! Some helpful locals show him the way to the police station.

Hergé kept a photo (shown below) of the Bosnian town of Mostar in his archives. Check out the red-tiled roofs and minarets. It looks like Mostar inspired Hergé's Syldavian village. Perhaps Syldavia is modeled on Bosnia?

Once upon a time...

Like Syldavia, many hundreds of years ago Bosnia was ruled by Slavic tribes. In the fifteenth century, the country was conquered by the Ottoman Empire. The Turkish conquest of Syldavia reflects this, although Hergé locates the event in the tenth century.

Further east

Yet while there are similarities between Bosnia and Syldavia, Romanian Tintin expert Dodo Niță believes that Syldavia is based on the Eastern European country of Romania.

Niță suggests that the name Syldavia is made up from the names of the two historical Romanian provinces of TranSYLvania and MolDAVIA. Romania is the only place in Europe where pelicans (the symbol of Syldavia) live in the wild. The brochure states that the Syldavian subsoil is rich in minerals; uranium deposits (which help Professor Calculus fly his atomic rocket built in Syldavia in *Destination Moon*) exist under the Carpathian Mountains in Romania.

For one more similarity, check out the portrait of King Muskar XII of Syldavia above a photo of Prince Alexandru Ioan Cuza (ruler of Romania, 1862–1866), then turn the page to **Explore and Discover!**

EXPLORE AND DISCOVER

Tintin has landed (with a bump!) in Syldavia. He has a hunch that sinister forces are plotting to steal the royal sceptre in an attempt to force the king to give up his throne. Tintin sets off for Klow, the capital of Syldavia, on a mission to warn the king, but is captured by a corrupt police official.

In the meantime, cunning imposter Alfred Alembick gains entrance to the Treasure Chamber at Kropow Castle by impersonating his brother, Professor Hector Alembick.

Just when we thought that we had considered every possible real country as the source of inspiration for Syldavia, we come across Kropow Castle, which is partly based on a real castle…in Finland!

OLAVINLINNA CASTLE

★ In 1475, Erik Axelsson Tott founded a fortress, Olavinlinna Castle, in the historical province of Savonia, in what is today Northern Europe.

★ At that time the region was part of the Swedish Kingdom; Olavinlinna Castle was located near the border with Russia in an effort to deter attacks by this country.

★ The castle became a center for trade, and in 1639 a town, Savonlinna, was founded around the castle.

★ The fortress has three stone towers, the design of which Hergé copied for Kropow Castle. These towers were built thick to withstand cannon fire.

★ Today Olavinlinna Castle hosts the annual Savonlinna Opera Festival, started in 1912 by Aino Ackté. Over the first four years of the festival, the only non-Finnish opera performed was Charles Gounod's *Faust* with its "Jewel Song," Bianca Castafiore's favorite aria! (Learn more about Bianca Castafiore on page 14!)

Ah! There's the palace!

In the story, Tintin arrives at the royal palace in Klow, Syldavia. Hergé based the palace on the real-life royal palace in Brussels, Belgium. In 1938, when Hergé was writing this story, Nazi Germany took over Austria. Belgians were worried that Belgium was next. Perhaps then Syldavia is meant to be Belgium under threat from its neighboring country (with Borduria in place of Germany in the story).

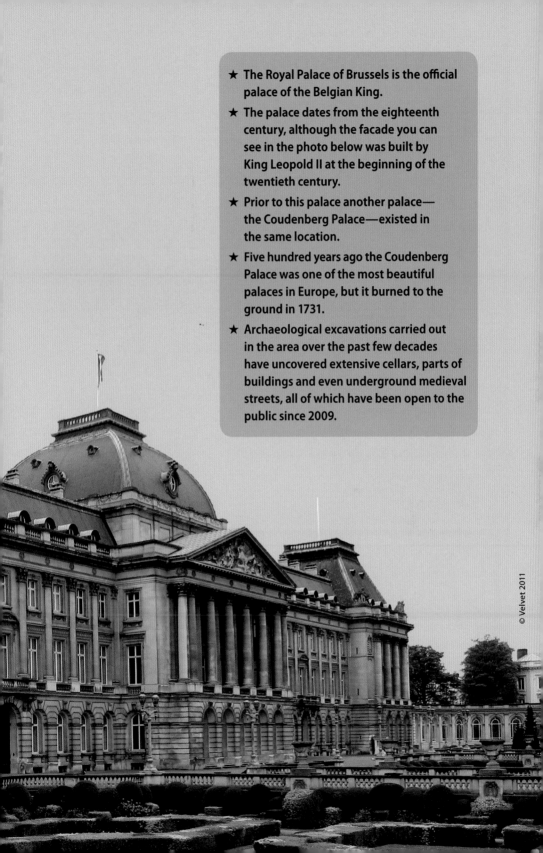

★ The Royal Palace of Brussels is the official palace of the Belgian King.

★ The palace dates from the eighteenth century, although the facade you can see in the photo below was built by King Leopold II at the beginning of the twentieth century.

★ Prior to this palace another palace—the Coudenberg Palace—existed in the same location.

★ Five hundred years ago the Coudenberg Palace was one of the most beautiful palaces in Europe, but it burned to the ground in 1731.

★ Archaeological excavations carried out in the area over the past few decades have uncovered extensive cellars, parts of buildings and even underground medieval streets, all of which have been open to the public since 2009.

BIANCA CASTAFIORE

Tintin makes it inside the royal palace only to interrupt a performance by the opera singer Bianca Castafiore!

This is the first time that Castafiore makes an appearance in The Adventures of Tintin. In later Tintin stories she is sometimes referred to by her stage name, "The Milanese Nightingale."

Although she may be, like all good divas, prone to vanity and swooning (Tintin's surprise entrance to the royal palace sees her promptly faint), Bianca Castafiore turns out to be a loyal and brave friend to Tintin and Captain Haddock, whose name she never pronounces correctly.

> I don't know why, but whenever I hear her it reminds me of a hurricane that hit my ship - when I was sailing in the West Indies some years ago . . .

But in the end Hergé leaves no room for doubt when it comes to his musical tastes: in this frame from The Seven Crystal Balls, he lets Captain Haddock speak on his behalf!

AN OPERA LEGEND

While Hergé may well have based Bianca Castafiore on opera singers in general, he was probably influenced by several real people in particular. For instance, when he was a young boy in the 1910s, his aunt would sing to the family when they visited at teatime.

But some people think that Hergé had a real opera singer in mind for Bianca Castafiore: Aino Ackté.

Ackté.

AINO ACKTÉ

★ Aino Ackté (1876–1944) was a Finnish opera singer born into a musical family.

★ Ackté was taught singing by her mother until she was accepted to study at the Paris Conservatory, a prestigious music school.

★ Aino Ackté's successful performance of Gounod's *Faust* in 1897, including the "Jewel Song" that Bianca Castafiore is always singing, earned her a six-year contract with the Paris Grand Opera.

★ In 1912, Ackté founded the Savonlinna Opera Festival, held at Olavinlinna Castle in Finland (see page 9).

★ Aino Ackté had a sister named Irma. In the later Tintin story *The Calculus Affair*, we are introduced to Bianca Castafiore's maid, also named Irma!

EUREKA!

The royal sceptre has been stolen! When walking past a toy shop, Tintin suddenly realizes how the thieves did it. He cries "Eureka!" in excitement, but why?

Sixteenth-century engraving showing Archimedes in his bath.

The ancient Greek mathematician Archimedes (287–212 B.C.) was asked to measure the purity of a gold crown. He realized that if he knew the volume of the crown he could calculate the purity of the gold. But the crown was not a regular shape, which made measuring the volume difficult. Then, when getting into the bathtub, Archimedes realized that water in the tub was displaced in exact proportion to the volume of his body in it. So he simply measured the water displaced by the crown with a measuring jug, which gave him the crown's volume. At this point he yelled "Eureka!" meaning "I've found it!" in ancient Greek. Ever since, the word has been associated with a sudden discovery or breakthrough.

ESCAPE FROM BORDURIA!

Tintin has retrieved the sceptre but now he is trapped in Borduria. There is only one thing for it: he commandeers a Bordurian fighter plane and takes off! Hergé drew Messerschmitt Bf-109 fighter planes for the Bordurian air force.

© Anto Blazevic

★ The Messerschmitt Bf-109, also known as the Me-109, was a fighter plane deployed by Germany in Word War II.

★ A total of 33,484 of these machines were built, making it the most widely produced fighter plane ever.

★ The aircraft was advanced for its time and was designed so that important parts, such as the engine and weapons, could easily be accessed and removed for maintenance.

★ Thick bulletproof armor protected the pilot and the fuel tanks—useful features in a fighter plane!

★ More powerful versions of the aircraft with enhanced features and rearranged weaponry were created over the years: the model in this photo is a Bf-109G.

THE ROYAL PROCESSION

Tintin manages to make it back to Syldavia and returns the sceptre to its rightful owner, King Muskar XII. The royal procession takes place on St. Vladimir's Day. The magnificent carriage is based on the British Royal Family's Gold State Coach. Hergé's archives include black-and-white pictures of the coach being used for the coronation of King George V in 1911, but you can see a splendid color photo of the coach on the right!

★ The Gold State Coach was built in 1762 in London.

★ The coach is decorated with lions' heads, cherubs, crowns, dolphins and palm trees, and is covered in gold leaf. The decoration also incorporates painted panels.

★ The coach is 23 feet long and 12 feet high, and weighs 4 tons. It needs at least 8 horses to pull it.

★ The Gold State Coach has been used for the coronation—the crowning ceremony— of every British monarch since King George IV in 1821.

To celebrate the royal procession, there is an exciting piece of treasure waiting for you on the next page: a partially-inked sketch by Hergé showing the interior of the royal palace at Klow.

Turn the page and check it out!

The Royal Collection © Her Majesty the Queen Elizabeth II

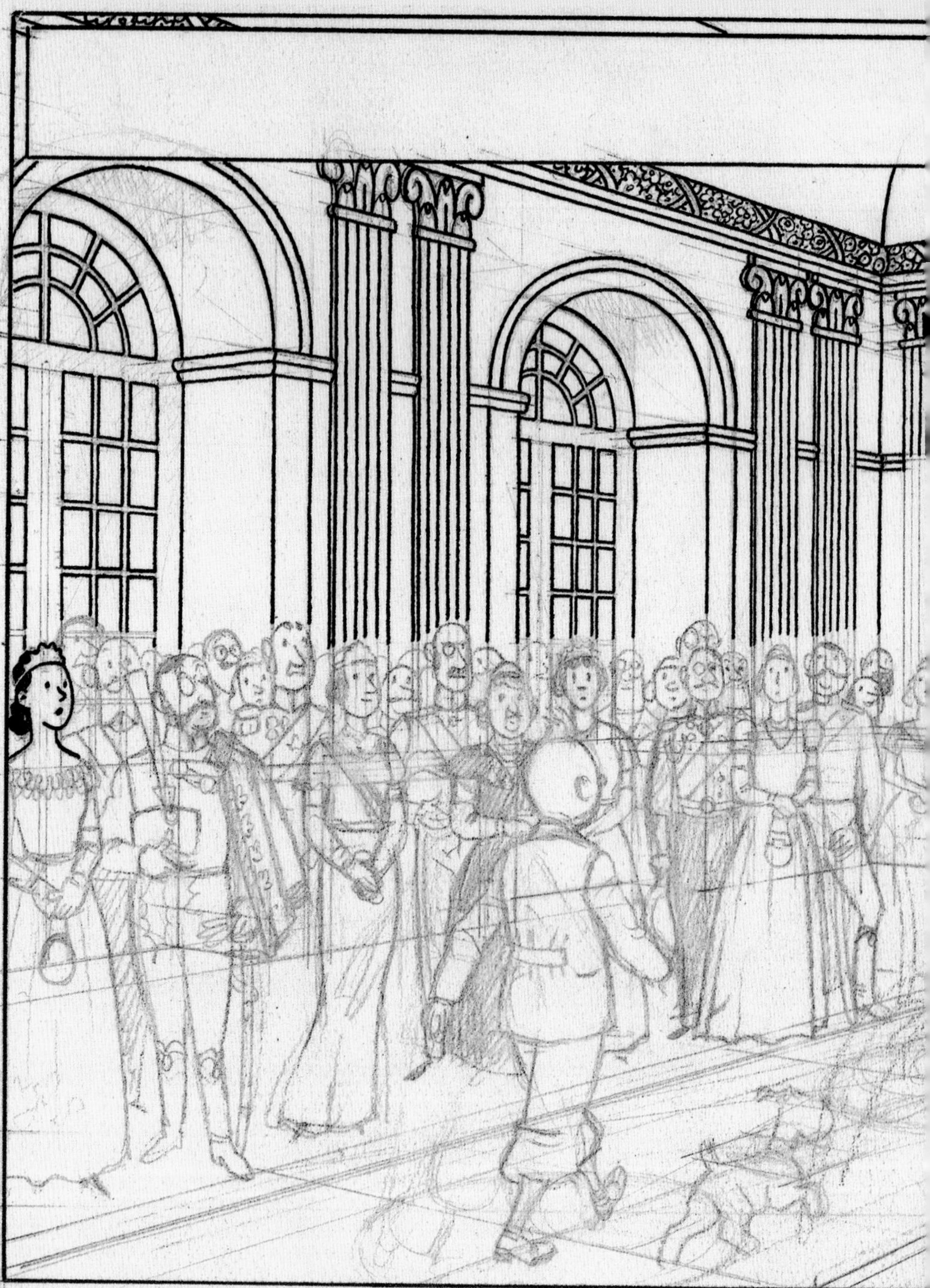

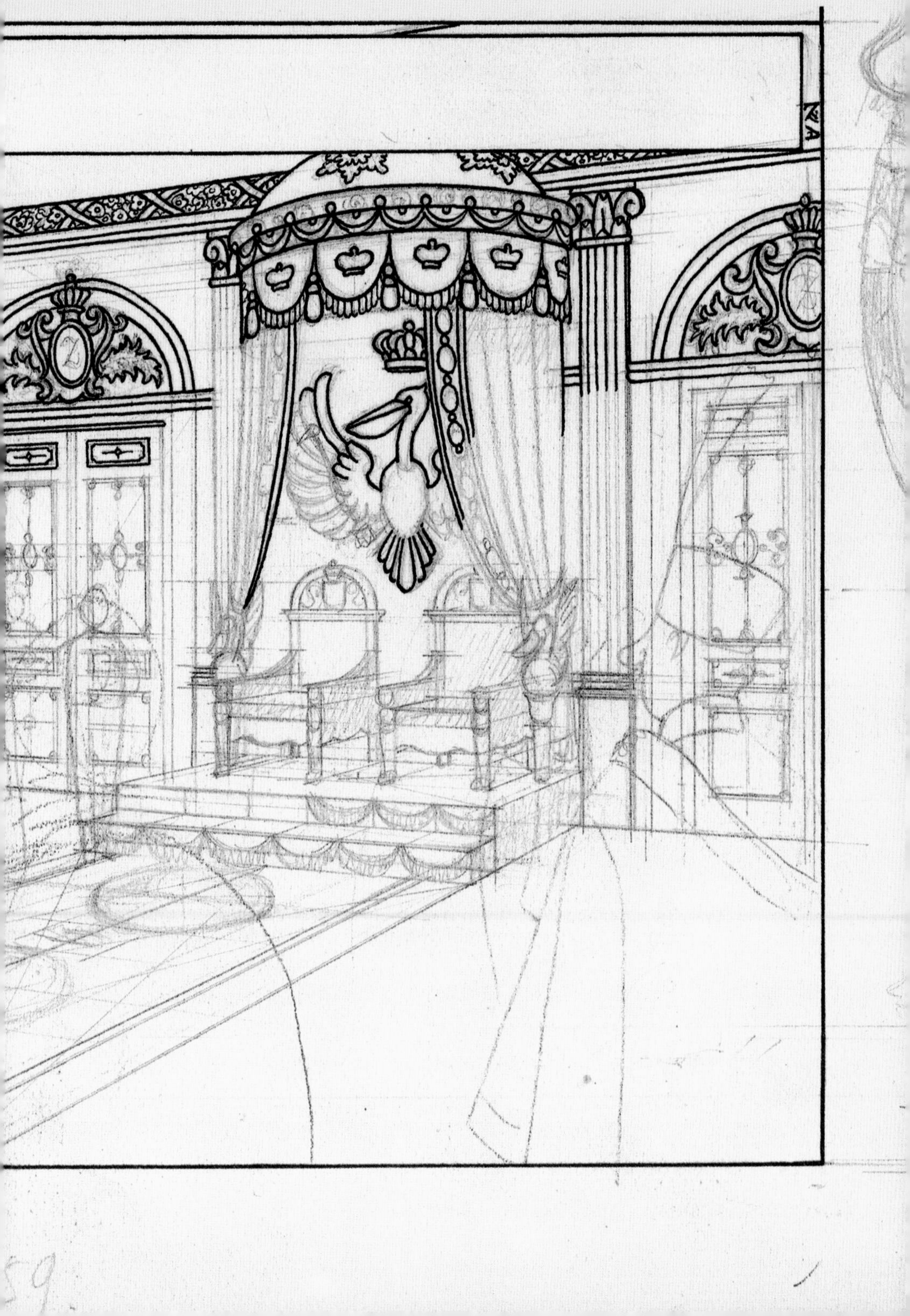

THE THRONE ROOM

The picture on the previous pages was not used in the final version of the story, but it provides a wonderful, early and rare example of a detailed pencil sketch that Hergé left partially inked in. In the end, however, the author chose to use the perspective shown below.

And now the King is once more in his palace. Time and again the delirious crowds have called His Majesty back on to the balcony to receive their tumultuous acclaim. But now he is seated here in the Throne Room, where an investiture is taking place . . .

FRIENDLY CROWDS

The story finishes in truly spectacular style: Tintin arrives to receive his knighthood as the royal court looks on.

Édouard
Cnaepelinckx

Jacques
Van Melkebeke

Marcel
Stobbaerts

Edgar Pierre
Jacobs

Paul Remi,
Germaine Kieckens
and Hergé

Hergé wanted to be present for the occasion…along with his friends! Can you spot them all in the crowd?

TINTIN'S GRAND ADVENTURE

When *King Ottokar's Sceptre* was first published, World War II was just beginning; by the end of May 1940, Belgium was occupied by Germany. Hergé was forced to make a decision. If he wanted to continue publishing Tintin stories he had to steer clear of political storylines! This was the beginning of a period during which strong themes of fantasy and exotic adventure emerged in Hergé's Tintin adventures.

Trivia: *King Ottokar's Sceptre*

Professor Alembick's collection of seals is comprehensive: experts now believe that the only known complete example of the seal of Edward the Confessor (1042–1066)—the first English monarch to use a seal—is a forgery.

For the color version of King Ottokar's Sceptre, published in 1947, Hergé embellished Kropow Castle by adding a tower from Vyborg Castle in Russia to those based on Olavinlinna Castle in Finland.

It appears that Hergé mixed elements from many sources when he created the fictional European country of Syldavia. It is so clever that we can't say he based it on just one place!

Hergé may have been inspired by elements from the movie The Prisoner of Zenda (1937). In the film, an Englishman who resembles the king of the fictional country of Ruritania pretends to be the king at his coronation in order to save the monarchy. So in the movie the look-alike is the good guy!

- Hergé -
les aventures de
TINTIN

LE SCEPTRE
D'OTTOKAR

CASTERMAN

The original cover for *King Ottokar's Sceptre* (1939)

GO ON MORE ADVENTURES WITH TINTIN!

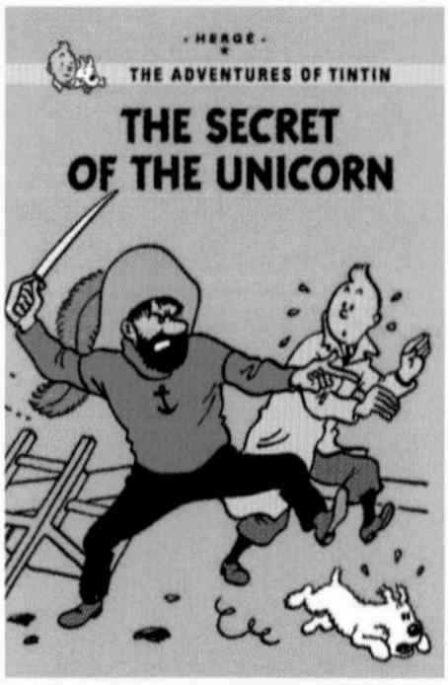
HERGÉ
THE ADVENTURES OF TINTIN
THE SECRET OF THE UNICORN

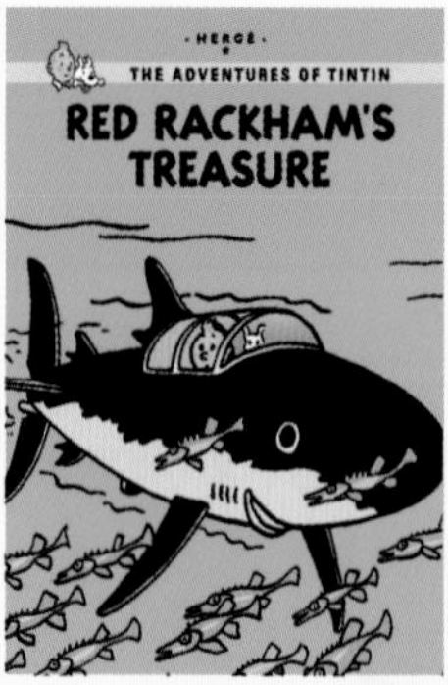
HERGÉ
THE ADVENTURES OF TINTIN
RED RACKHAM'S TREASURE

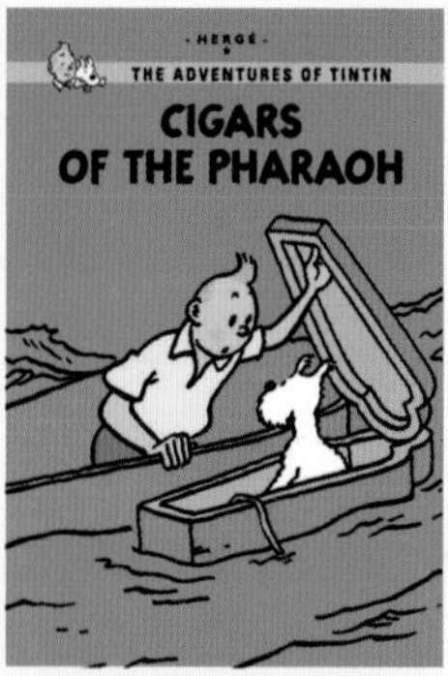
HERGÉ
THE ADVENTURES OF TINTIN
CIGARS OF THE PHARAOH

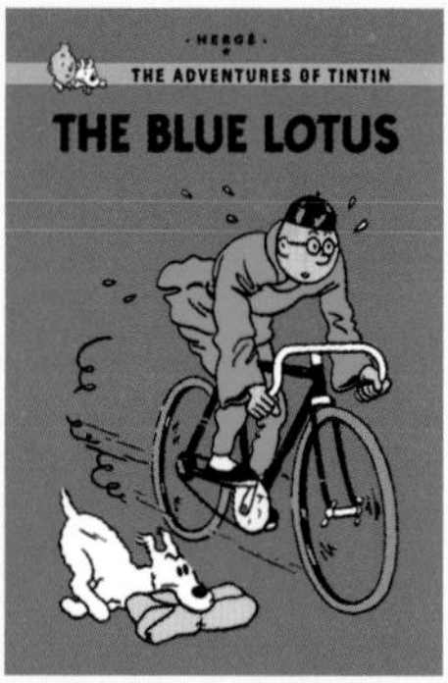
HERGÉ
THE ADVENTURES OF TINTIN
THE BLUE LOTUS

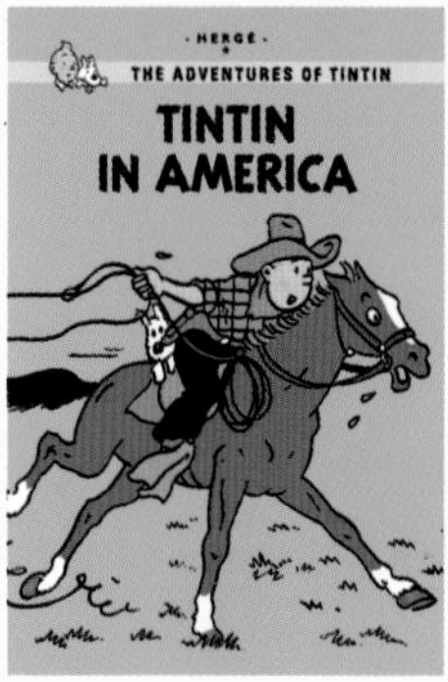
HERGÉ
THE ADVENTURES OF TINTIN
TINTIN IN AMERICA

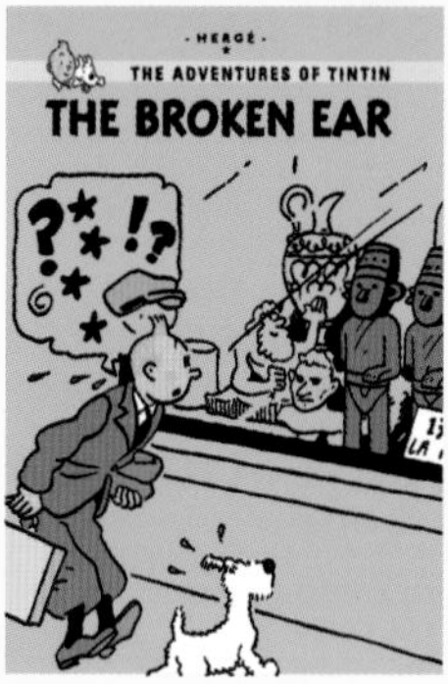
HERGÉ
THE ADVENTURES OF TINTIN
THE BROKEN EAR

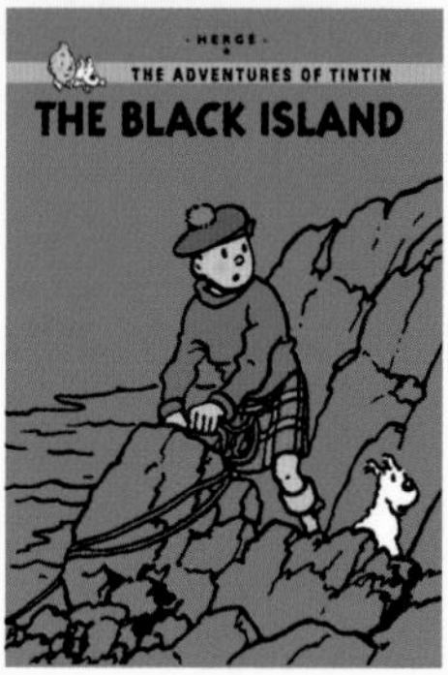
HERGÉ
THE ADVENTURES OF TINTIN
THE BLACK ISLAND

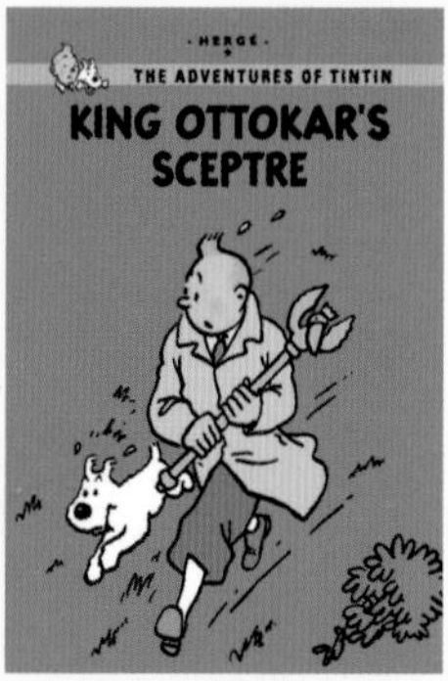
HERGÉ
THE ADVENTURES OF TINTIN
KING OTTOKAR'S SCEPTRE

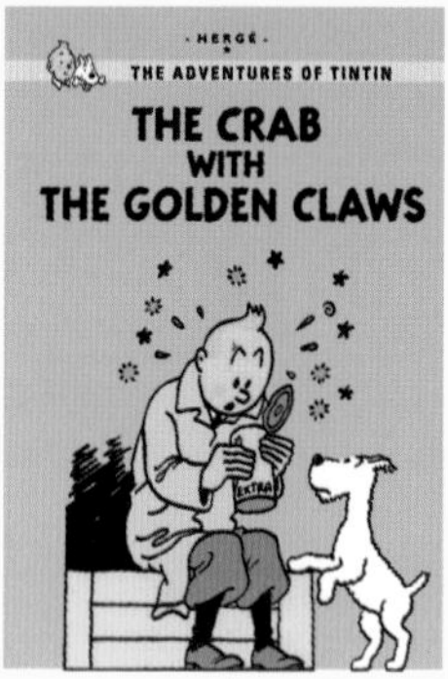
HERGÉ
THE ADVENTURES OF TINTIN
THE CRAB WITH THE GOLDEN CLAWS

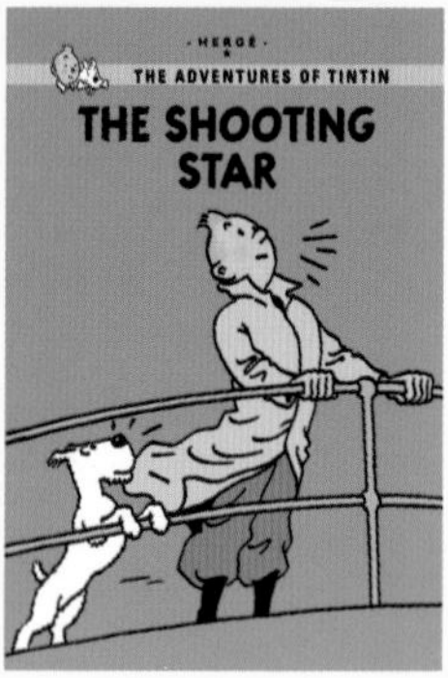
HERGÉ
THE ADVENTURES OF TINTIN
THE SHOOTING STAR

ALSO AVAILABLE

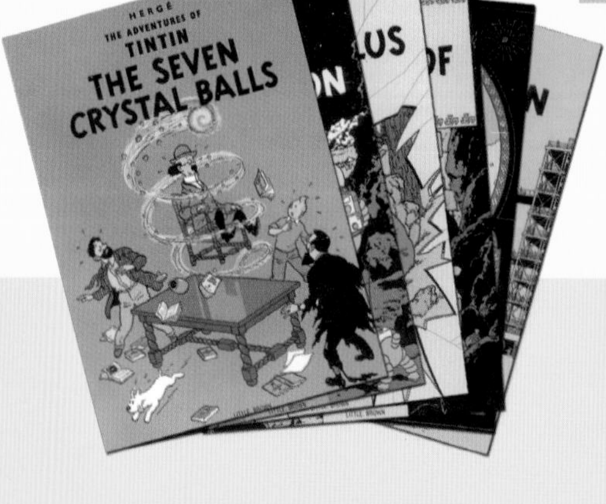
HERGÉ
THE ADVENTURES OF TINTIN
THE SEVEN CRYSTAL BALLS

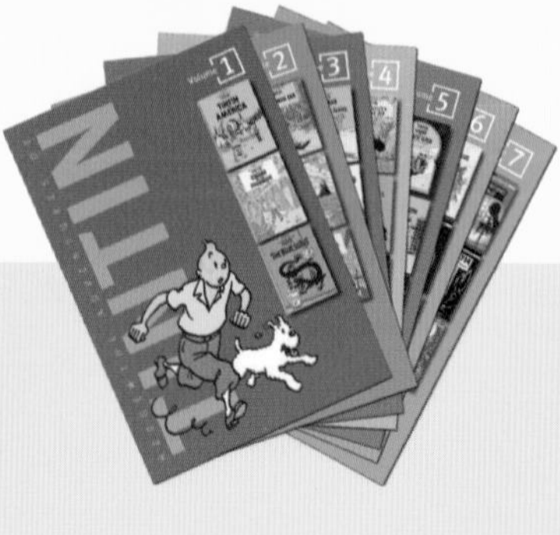
1
2
3
4
5
6
7